LUNA STATION QUARTERLY

ISSUE 023
SEPTEMBER 2015

EDITOR & PUBLISHER
Jennifer Lyn Parsons

ASSISTANT EDITORS
Tara Calaby
Cathrin Hagey
Andi Marquette
Megan Patton
Danielle Perry
Iona Sharma

COVER ARTIST
Erin DeMoss

LUNA STATION PRESS

First Paperback Edition September 2015
ISBN: 978-1-938697-68-5

Luna Station Quarterly publishes short fiction on March 1st, June 1st,
September 1st, and December 1st. For more information and submission
guidelines, please visit our website at lunastationquarterly.com

For Luna Station Press
Creative Director - Tara Quinn Lindsey

LUNA STATION PRESS
576 Valley Road #197
Wayne, NJ 07470
www.lunastationpress.com
info@lunastationpress.com

CONTENTS

EDITORIAL
JENNIFER LYN PARSONS

"The beginning is always today." ~ Mary Shelley

I've been thinking quite a bit lately about stories and storytelling. Surprise, surprise, right? Specifically, I've been thinking about how there is a very gendered divide in people's reactions to the kinds of stories that are out there.

Now, I'm no stranger to this phenomenon. When I started out in my writing career, I started in fan fiction. No shame there, I learned the nuts and bolts of how to write by churning out stories about Obi-Wan. Fandom is a great, supportive community for new writers.

The thing that really popped out at me during that experience, and the reason I founded LSQ in the first place, is that I found that the vast majority of writers in fan fiction are women. And the vast majority of stories are heavily character driven. There are still lightsabers and spaceships, daring rescues and hardened soldiers doing battle across the stars, or across the fantastical environment of your choice. But there is a lot more emphasis put on how these events effect the participants emotionally. Yes, up to and including how they fall and love and who is on the recieving end of that love. I was getting stories in fandom the like of which never saw the light of day in official publications.

That was a long time ago for me. Fast-forward to now and I finally managed to get into video games, and the world of Dragon Age specifically. The first and third game have wide, sweeping epic stories, huge battles, the fate of the world is in your hands and you seem to be the "Chosen One", leading everyone around you through this "Dark Time". I love these games because along with the pretty graphics and all, there are some great stories being told, with really solid characters. Very "Star Wars" in scope.

You may note that I mentioned the first and third games. That's because the second game is decidedly different.

Instead of ranging all over, you mostly stay in one town. Instead of being the "Chosen One", you're a refugee pulling yourself up by your bootstraps. Instead of having companions willing to follow you everywhere, you have a group of friends who sometimes disagree with your choices and even leave you permanently. In other words, the characters and their development are the focal point of the game.

While the first and third installments were heaped with praise, the second came under a lot of fire. Yes, some of the criticism was valid, the mechanics themselves are a bit repetitive at times, but the story was largely panned as not being epic enough, not "important" enough to be worth playing through.

At least that was how a lot of men saw it.

One glance through the threads of various forums and the gender divide became exceedingly obvious. Men found the whole game dull and women largely felt engrossed by the characters and their stories and loved it. A little poking around Tumblr reveals exactly how much these characters are loved.

Men were put off by the romance, the flirting, and probably most offensively of all, the look of the warrior woman friend of the main character, a personal favorite of mine. She was criticised for not being "pretty" enough. She was lovely, to my eyes, and had true personality, not blending in with all the other cookie cut out pretty women in the game. There have been "modifications" made for the game by fans that change her face, make her "pretty". And this is for a character that you don't even get to romance. They just didn't like the look of her.

All this in a game that is rife with battles, random violence and plenty of foul-mouthed sexual innuendo, features that are consistent with other similar games that guys loved.

The dividing line, intriguingly, was in how the characters were written and their story arcs. I'm not sure what to even make of that. What is it about our cultural gender divide that makes women more likely to gravitate toward games, toward stories, that focus more on character details and interactions? Even when, as far as violence, language, and sexual content go, they are on par with stories that have a more epic scope? And what is it about these kind of stories that turn men off from them?

In thinking about this, I find myself asking more questions than finding answers. Are there any companies out there that are taking note of this divide? Is anyone working to publish more books, comics, media, and games that use characters and their development the way so many women would like to see them used? Are there companies, established or new, that are willing to push in these directions?

Most importantly, where can we find and support these new voices? I don't believe this is something that will naturally work itself out. I think this requires women to ask for what they want, to talk to developers at cons, to write emails to the big companies, to continue to support places that provide a home for the kind of stories we want to see in the world.

And when possible, to write and draw and build those kinds of stories, comics, and games ourselves. There is a vast, obviously untapped audience out there that well and truly does want to watch deeply felt, well-developed characters triumph over all the evil in their path and then kiss their partner-in-arms, blood-spattered armor be damned.

LSQ·023

HIS SOUL

CATHRIN HAGEY

Cathrin Hagey is a writer, blogger, and editor based in the Canadian prairies. Among her favorite things: family, dogs, primal grasslands, the Canadian Shield, containers, plant-human hybrids, San Francisco, and an LoTR collectible plaque signed by Virginia Lee. Her work has appeared in New Fairy Tales, Luna Station Quarterly, Kind of a Hurricane Press, Huffington Post, and elsewhere.

Who looks outside, dreams; who looks inside, awakes.

—C.G. Jung

Long ago, a young king, having gone abroad in the guise of a peasant, more for his amusement than his edification, wandered off the beaten path and plunged into a wood in search of meat and drink.

He was soon rewarded for his foolhardy courage with a whiff of vapor-freshened air, and then, in another half-league or so, with the silver voice of a swift-moving stream. The swiftness might have given him pause, since he was as far from the mountains as one could get in this kingdom, but the prince was too thirsty to reflect upon that.

He cupped the water in his hands, as any gentleman would, at first, and when the depth of his need was revealed to him, he went in face first and slurped like a common cur. Nothing had ever satisfied him as much.

The king was in a water-induced reverie when he saw her— a young woman, perhaps his own age, perhaps older. She quickly slipped behind a tree, her shabby gown blinking once as she disappeared.

The hunt was on. His blood was up. The king didn't pause to consider whether the maid was frightened of him, or whether she was maid at all. His inclination was to give chase.

She sprang from her tree, bolted over a grassy mound, and splashed across the stream, falling and dragging herself up the opposite bank. The king followed, and soon came upon her, upright and leaning against the trunk of a massive oak.

Her eyes were wide open, and from her pallor, and the state of her dress, which was badly torn and thin enough to show her knobby knees, he surmised that she was half-starved.

For the first time since he'd ventured beyond his castle walls, the king was sorry he had. The adventure he'd imagined didn't include discovering a maid, especially one such as this.

She blinked her somber eyes at him. Her chest rose and fell beneath filthy rags.

"Do you know who I am?" the king asked.

The maid stared at him. He wondered at her boldness in not answering at once.

"What is your name?"

She lowered herself to a cushion of moss at the foot of the tree and wrapped her arms around her bare legs.

The king looked around him for assistance, from habit. But there was nothing and no one, only thick woods and occasional scurrying sounds from within and around the trees. He considered walking away as though he had never seen her; he didn't know what held him there.

The king found that her eyes mastered him in a manner he did not comprehend.

"Where are your people?"

She reached out her arms and opened and closed her hands in a way that suggested to him she would have his cloak. And when the king removed the garment and held it out to her, she took it, and lay down, covering her own soiled flesh with it.

For three days the king fed her water from his own hands, kept her warm with his cloak, and sang to her the songs he had learned at his nurse's knee, that good woman who would have been more astonished than anyone to find her former charge attending to the needs of another.

At dawn on the fourth day, the maid sat up. The cloak fell to her waist as she reached for the leg of rabbit the king held out for her.

"You must tell me who you are?" he said, thinking that she might very well be what rather than who.

She held the meat between her hands, as a squirrel handles an acorn, and smiled dumbly. The king sat down beside her, unaware that he twinned her manner of sitting.

"Now that you're feeling better, you must tell me who you are, or at least where you came from."

The maid nibbled on the rabbit leg, soundlessly.

It was in that moment that the king decided to end his forest sojourn for good. He wanted nothing more than a hearty supper, a great silver goblet of wine, and his lover's bed. The filthy maid, dumb and of unknown origin, was not fit to return with him. He beamed his false reassurance with a smile. She returned the smile, and he saw that her fathomless eyes held light.

It was only a matter of stepping away. She could keep the cloak.

The maid picked at the bone with her teeth, in the manner of a doe nibbling grass, not at all like a ravening creature. When she appeared satisfied that no meat was left, she lowered her hands to her lap and fixed her eyes on the king. He hoped that she would speak, but she did not.

He wanted only to turn and quickly regain the road home, but found that he could not leave her. There was something there—not helplessness nor boldness—something older, deeper, darker, fairer, that made him want to crush her to his own breast, in a gesture both wild and tender. Never before had anyone stirred such a feeling in him, a feeling not bounded by love, hate, desire, or anything he knew.

"Are you well enough to journey?"

The king pried the leg bone from her hands and threw it away. Then he raised her to her feet, slowly. She trembled at first, and then appeared to take strength from him as he held her. When he sensed that she was steady enough, the king led her forward for several steps.

"If you are, I'll take you to my castle. It's not a long way, as the crow flies, but it will be several days before we see the turrets through the trees."

***

The king ordered servants to bathe and dress the maid and then sought his bride in her chamber. He seldom went to her, except to pay her the respect that was her due, the maintenance of her dignity. He hoped the freshly washed maid would soon keep her company, freeing him to keep his elsewhere.

He took precautions to have the maid tutored in the artful manners of a courtier, and plumped with sweets and meat, before releasing her into the company of his bride. When the hour of introduction arrived, he endeavored to do the thing himself.

"Look what I have brought for you, my love."

The queen was draped in an indigo sheath that caught light along the curvature of her thighs. She dropped her smile upon spying the maid. "What is that?"

"A gift."

The king led the maid to a low seat from where the queen could clearly survey the offering. "She was abandoned. I found her during my wandering—half dead."

The queen smiled at the king, but any warmth in it failed to reach him. "A maid for a present," she mused. "And she is mine? I may do anything I like with her?"

The king quickly disabused her of such a notion. "She is a poor soul in need of care."

The queen leaned forward and ran her fingers through the maid's dark hair. "She's not hideous. I wonder what defect in her led to her abandonment." She paused. "And I wonder what made you believe I would want her?"

All this time, the maid sat quietly on the seat, her back bent slightly, her eyes staring straight ahead, seeming not to listen to either speaker, until the queen addressed her directly. "I think I've seen you before…once."

The maid said nothing, but she fixed her dark eyes on the queen's, and her lips curled a little at the corners.

"Ah ha," warbled the queen. There's a spirit inside her."

The king kneeled across from the maid and looked into her eyes.

"What do you see?" said the queen.

The king dared not tell his bride the truth—in one of the maid's storm cloud eyes he saw himself as child, left to cry himself to sleep; in the other, he appeared old, weakened, gasping for air. He said, "I see—"

"Witch? Nymph? Your mad sister?" The queen twitched with laughter. Then, without another word, she retreated along the hall, lifting as she did so her sheath to show the form beneath, the snow of her bare skin to compare with the cherry of the king's cheek.

The king rallied his wits, took the maid by the hand, and retreated to his lover's quarters.

***

The bed curtains parted as soon as the king bolted the heavy door from the inside. A smooth, brown nose jutted through.

"I've brought someone," said the king

The king's lover showed his face through the curtains. His eyes were wide as he stared at the wisp of a maid at the king's side. "What is that?"

"You mean, *who* is that? You're beginning to sound like the queen."

The lover stepped down from the bed to reveal two firm, shapely legs, and a torso bare except for a strip of linen tied at the waist.

The king let go of the maid and took his lover's hands in his own. "I found her in the woods—alone. She was abandoned." He sighed and waited for his lover's affirmation of his heroics.

"Why do you still have *it*?"

"Don't speak if you're going to be cruel." The king knew how to assert his authority when necessary, and defending his decision to save the maid felt necessary, though he struggled to comprehend why.

"She was starved, likely beaten, and perhaps—" he hesitated to say it—"defiled. Where is your heart?"

Somewhat chastened, and in need of the king's comforting arms, the lover refined his notes. Stepping toward her, he placed the palm of one hand against the maid's cheek. "So soft, for a peasant. Like milk. Or water." He stroked her neck with both palms. "She's lovely. What's her name?

"I don't know. She doesn't speak."

"Marvelous!" cried the lover. "We can imagine all sorts of things—she's a creature of the woods, a mythical beast, a spirit—a sprite!" He pinched the girl's cheeks and then threw himself on the bed and roared like a lion.

The king was unnerved to discover that the depth of his desire to protect the maid seemed greater than his need to soothe his lover.

The lover rolled onto his back and tore off the strip of linen.

He tossed it at the king. "I knew you'd lose your wits out there in the woods."

"Be decent, for her sake."

"Get rid of her—for my sake!"

"Where will she go?"

"Wherever the wind takes her." The lover pulled the king, whose limbs had loosened along with his will, into bed.

The maid lay on the floor and went to sleep.

***

Morning came, and the king awakened to find the maid naked as a plucked peahen, her breasts as aroused as the ears of a dog, stroking the hairs on his chest. His first impulse was to lie still and enjoy the sensation, but he soon came to his senses.

"What?" called the lover. "Where are you going?"

But the king was too busy dressing the maid, and his own skin, to pay heed.

The lover lifted the sheet to reveal his desire. Again, he said, "Where are you going?"

The king didn't know where he was going. He only knew that he must breathe some other air, alone. And alone meant something new.

"Wait for me," cried the lover, but the king took the maid by the hand and unbolted the door. They moved lightly and swiftly through a narrow passage, down stairs, down more stairs, and through the great castle doors.

As he walked with the maid into the world beyond the castle walls, in the direction of the wood where he first found her, the king muttered to himself: "By what right did I enfold this creature within my own home, my own bosom? Who am I to go abroad, wandering hither and yon, casting my net into the sea of being and dragging in whatever thing caught there? What manner of thing have I caught?"

For days he walked, the maid at his side, silent yet present, her companionship no longer a burden on him, as if he had carved her from bone or wood with his own hands, breathed life into her, and pulled her into his.

Surely, he had not.

Sooner than the king expected, he heard the silver voice of the swift-moving stream from which he, once, greedily drank. Then they came upon the midden of rabbit bones and the place where he had fed her. The king knew not what came next.

"Go where you will," he said to the maid, to the wind, to the water.

The maid embraced him. He held onto her as firmly as she held him. Then she let go and gestured for him to follow her.

They had walked a league when then the maid stepped forward and dropped into a hidden spring, vanishing into the velvet depth of it.

The king jumped forward and reached out with his hand, but he grasped nothing. He searched for her, expecting to see froth where life fought to prevail, but the surface was a looking glass.

For one brief spell, he thought he saw her pale face, the two dark eyes like stones, the hair a mass of stirring weed. Then she disappeared, and in her stead the king found the planes and contours of his own face reflected in the deep pool.

And though, ever afterward, the king would appear to adore his own reflection, interminably, in truth, it was not so.

ELEUSINIAN MYSTERIES

CHARLOTTE ASHLEY

Charlotte Ashley is a writer, editor, critic, and bookseller in Toronto, Canada. Her work has appeared The Magazine of Fantasy & Science Fiction, The Sockdolager, Kaleidotrope, and a number of anthologies. Her bookish ramblings can be found at www.once-and-future.com.

Her moon was almost done. Maghfira blew ruddy copper spirals off the newly-carved plate, examining the curves and grooves she had spent the last ten hours engraving. It was not the moon that hung over Amsterdam, but the other side. Hatched with mountains, upside-down and plump as a peach, only the verges suggested familiar landmarks. This moon's face was a vast expanse of fanciful topography, including a city on the north-western edge of the Oceanus Procellarum—*Eleusis*.

She had just taken up her graver again when two men entered her shop without knocking. Maghfira squinted from where she sat hunched over her desk, her eyes watery and sore from the hours spent sketching by dim rushlights. For a moment, the crosshatched lines of her project remained burned into her eyes, framing the men in an alien landscape of mountains and oceans, stars and cities.

They were men from the *Vereenigde Oost-Indische Compagnie*—Dutch East India Company—she was sure. Either that or smugglers, though they amounted to the same thing in the Dutch Republic. The bulkier of the two men waited by the door while the second, a wide-faced, bearded fellow dressed cap to toe in black, perused the sketches, frames and supplies that littered her print shop.

"Hello?" she asked. "Can I help you?"

"Where is your master, *Blauwe*?" he asked her without making eye contact, rifling through the prints stacked on her small press. The insult sharpened Maghfira's senses, clearing her starry daydreams with a cold flush of fear.

"I am the mistress here," she declared, laying aside her graver and standing. "I'm Maghfira van Delsen. What is your business?"

"You?" The man smirked and finally looked at her. "Coloured Hollander, are you? Van Delsen's a Dutch name. Your daddy had a good time in Batavia, I see."

Maghfira balled her hands into fists and tried to calm her mounting temper. She might be Dutch by law, but there would always be oafs who only saw her Javanese blood. It was, however, the first time someone had come right into her shop to insult her to her face. She told herself to be cautious, as these men were big and her serving girl, Arjani, was still at market.

"What is your business?" she repeated slowly.

"Last week you were delivered a cartload of engravings. Maps," the man said, roaming the cramped room. "From Mr. Janssonius."

Maghfira paused. "Yes," she eventually replied, unable to fathom what a large and rude VOC man could possibly care about a simple repair job. She barely cared herself. The plates from Janssonius' *Harmonia Macrocosmica* had already been printed hundreds of times over by the time she had gotten her hands on them. She was copying them now that the originals had been flattened and worn by repeated impressions. It was rote work, but the best she could get. Despite her efforts, nobody had commissioned any original work from her. She was known for her copyist's skills and for her infallible memory. Maghfira van Delsen: *fake engraver, fake Hollander.*

"Are these them?" The man started browsing through the racks of wood-framed plates leaning against the walls.

"Excuse me!" Maghfira pushed to his side, appalled. "This is a private commission, thank you. Now I ask you again…" she tried to insert her slight self between this man and the plates, "…do please state your business, or get out. I have work to do."

The man frowned suspiciously at her and refused to back away. With her nose very nearly pressed to his waistcoat, she could smell ink, smoke and herring in the fine black of his clothes, see cunning in his bloodshot eyes. She held his gaze defiantly. *I am mistress here. Me.*

"Show me the maps, mistress," he said, with cold efficiency.

Maghfira's thoughts raced. She could scream, and perhaps old van Laer next door would come to her aid, though he had never liked her much. By instinct and habit she wanted to lock wills with this man, but she could not ignore how he towered over her, how his big, calloused hands could encircle her throat, were he so inclined. She reluctantly stepped aside.

The man flipped through all twenty-nine plates in seconds, pulling them away from the wall and examining the space behind. He let them fall back with a clatter and turned back to her.

"Are there any others?" he asked.

The question hung between them for a moment too long. *Ah,* Maghfira thought. *Is that what this is about? You want Eleusis.*

She had known there was something different about that last plate, its copper rosy and fresh, its lines cut sharp and new. It wasn't from Janssonius' atlas; it wasn't from any book yet printed. It must have been gathered up by accident when they had loaded the cart. That was why she had pulled it aside, kept it for herself. It was too fantastical for a serious work of uranography, but just familiar enough to her. It filled her with nostalgia for the huge, upside-down moons of her childhood, lustrous with dreams.

"No," she stammered, a surge of possessiveness overcoming her. "This is all of them."

It was a bad lie, and the man looked beyond her, over her shoulder towards her desk and her kitchen. "Tell me truthfully, mistress, for if I think you are lying, I will burn this house to the ground." Maghfira had no cause to doubt his words. She looked down, suppressing the urge to spit in his eye.

"No," she whispered. "There are no more."

"Look at me!" he ordered, and she did. *Let him see fear,* she hoped. *They always mistake fear for submission.*

The man studied her a moment, then scowled. "How can anyone read anything in those squinted eyes of yours?" he demanded. "You look like a liar, *Blauwe.*" He pushed past her.

Maghfira flinched. Prints and sketches of the moon-map were scattered haphazardly around her desk, pinned, smudged and dusted with metal shavings. In the centre of it all, her perfect copy, newly engraved and lacking only the last details. The man took the plate in one great hand, studied it a moment, and then tucked it under his arm.

"That's mine!" she blustered as he gathered the sketches up as well. "My work, my own—" She bit her tongue as the man started fishing through her cabinet and turned up the original she had been copying. "I wasn't forging it," she insisted, excuses spilling from her lips in panic as she trailed the man around the room. His silence was more alarming than a denunciation would have been. "It was only for me, just to look at. I was going to return the plate to Janssonius."

"I don't give a *penningen* about Janssonius," the man said without looking at her, over-filling her hearth with the rumpled papers.

"What are you doing?" Maghfira demanded, alarmed. The man returned to her desk in silence, retrieving a large bottle of correcting acid and the last stub of a lit rush. "Stop it, you can't—no!" Laying the moon-plate atop the prints, he doused the heap in acid and applied the touch of the wick. Maghfira shielded her eyes as the pile exploded into flames and filaments of orange smoke, spilling on to the stone as the fire collapsed. She ran to stamp the loose leaves into the stone, choking on the nauseating fumes sizzling off the copper plates. She grabbed at the man as he pushed past her with a lit tinder, but he shrugged her off like a cloak.

"You should not have lied to me, Mistress *Blauwe*. You have betrayed the animal cunning of your people," he continued with calm. He carefully lit the sheets of paper draped over the bed of her small press, instigating a lively fire enthusiastically taken up by the woodwork of the machine that had cost her everything her father had left her. Maghfira cried at that, an angry, animal yell that made the man nod with satisfaction before leaving, shutting the door behind him.

Maghfira threw herself at the burning press, trying to smother the flames with damp paper and ink, but the mounting inferno was too well-fed. The noxious miasma of burning acid drove her from the house, shouting and crying for help. The neighbours brought bucket after bucket up from the canals to quell the flames, but there was little they could do. They shook their heads and tutted, as the last of her belongings smouldered inside the stone building like a kiln, as if she were a child who had dropped a sticky treat in the sand and not an independent woman who had just lost her livelihood to incomprehensible malice.

After a day and night spent fighting a losing battle against the fire, after the neighbours had given up and everything had been lost, Maghfira stood alone on her threshold with her petticoats blackened and reeking, seething with anger and confusion.

Her home, her press, her comforts, and her responsibilities. She had lost everything.

Not everything, she reminded herself as the moon dimmed with the coming of the day. *Amsterdam still holds my heart.*

She felt like a ship in a storm, tethered precariously by one last rope. She prayed it was strong enough to hold her fast.

***

If Constantin will not marry me now, Maghfira brooded, *I am lost.*

She started the long walk across town to Holfwijck, her lover's manor, as soon as daylight allowed it. The city was still waking as she crossed the wide lawn on foot, her serving girl having been returned to her family the night before. Maghfira could no longer afford to change her clothes, let alone pay poor, stunned Arjani.

Her affairs should have been settled by now. She had the training, background, experience, and talent to be a cartographer of the first order, but in the mercantile world of the VOC these virtues meant less than nothing. What she needed were the contacts, something a newcomer just off a ship from Batavia had too few of. She had taken her first jobs forging the work of more accomplished engravers thinking it would lead to more legitimate work, but in the eyes of the Dutch printers there was nothing legitimate about her.

She tried to turn down the *Harmonia Macrocosmica* job, but her broker, Bartelsz, had pressed her into it. "You need the income, Maggie," he'd told her, chewing his moustache and fixing her with a disapproving look. "Unless you've finally decided to return to Batavia, and your mother. I can find you a ship, dear girl. I think you've proved your point. Go home, before you've wasted all your father's hard-earned money."

That had made her angry enough to take even the pettiest commission, just to spite the old man. *Go home, indeed!* Batavia was not her home, just as it hadn't been her father's home. She was an independent woman now, with her own house, business and servant.

Or, at least, she had been, until yesterday.

"My lord Huygens says he will meet you in the kitchens," said Eelke, Constantin's nervous majordomo, glancing across the grass as if someone might see her. "It is indiscreet, you understand…" Maghfira steeled herself with fury, aware that if she succumbed to any calming measures she would drop from exhaustion.

"Eelke, how could you be so heartless? Your master wrote to me just last week, asking me to see him."

"Yes, mistress, but not *here*. Cross the canal, come the back way…" He blocked the entrance as effectively as a broom resting on a doorframe, and Maghfira could feel him slipping with each step she mounted.

"I'm here now, damn you, Eelke! Tell your master he will meet me in the library this minute, or by the Heavens, I will get on the first ship to Batavia without another word! My lord Constantin will see me now or he will never see me again!" She was nose to nose with the man now, and he folded completely. He stepped back to admit her, wringing his moist hands.

"You should not come alone, you see, and without a carriage…" he babbled as he trailed her resolute path towards the second-floor library.

"My servant is on errands, Eelke," she muttered, coming at last to the deep green room she knew so intimately. "And as for a carriage, you can tell my lord I blame him entirely for failing to provide me with one." She settled into the seat at Constantin's desk. "I will wait." She dismissed the servant.

She allowed herself a small sob of fatigue when Eelke left. The warm leather of the chair she had read so many books in lulled her into a sleepy melancholy. It was too easy to forget she did not belong here, that she was not—yet—Constantin's wife. Her fingers found the little box where Constantin kept the spectacles that fit so perfectly on the curved bridge of her nose. The relief to her sore eyes was instantaneous and almost put her to sleep. *Wake up, foolish girl!* she chided herself.

She drew a shaky breath and ran her fingers along the spines of Constantin's books to calm her nerves. A cabinet by the windows shelved newer works of mathematics and astronomy, along with an assortment of instruments and failed experiments. On the bottom shelf were several newly-bound books in English, which made her pause. Though she knew little enough of the language, she could make out bits of the titles. *The Man in the Moon,* read one. *A World in the Moon,* read another. She immediately opened the cabinet and removed them all.

They were bound in Flemish-green morocco like the rest of the Huygens collection, gold-tooled, each worth more than Maghfira could make in a year. The first book fell naturally to a folded insert sewn between two quires, its new hinge still stiff. She couldn't help but squawk with indignation when the map revealed itself to her.

It was her moon, the moon she had unwittingly traded for her home. Hand-drawn this time, the roads and canals of the city imagined in a different pattern, as if the same idea had been described to a different artist, but in all other ways so similar. The city was set in the same location at the edge of the moon's greatest sea, the grand avenues exiting at the same angles. The topography of the seas and mountains, the bestial constellations dancing about its sky, and the name: Eleusis. Her moon.

"Maggie," Constantin's subdued voice greeted her. Maghfira let the book tumble from her fingers as she turned towards him. He looked as tired as she felt, half-dressed in black stockings and a rumpled shirt. "What are you doing here? I haven't—that is, I was just writing to you. You've anticipated me, I'm afraid." He allowed a small, sheepish smile. Maghfira's belly turned over.

"Anticipated you? I certainly hope you weren't coming to call on me dressed like that," she teased him gently, covering her nerves with false coquetry. She had known it would surprise Constantin to see her alone and unannounced, but something in his manner told her she was not simply unexpected, but unwanted.

"No, I—" he stopped, and thought. "That is, I could give you the letter now. Perhaps we'd better start there."

"Yes, perhaps you had better," she replied quietly. He disappeared and returned with a folded sheaf of paper, which he handed to her hesitantly, as if he were afraid to get within arm's reach. Maghfira suddenly felt she didn't even need to read the letter, but she forced herself to anyway.

"Paris?" she read aloud, still scanning the page. "You're going to Paris—*a suitable wife?*" Her voice rose as she read the words, rage winning the war against desperation for control over her mood. "Constantin Huygens! What are you saying?"

He raised his hands defensively, eyes wide with alarm. "Maggie, my heart! You know I would not give you up for anything in the world. I love you. This is only—only a business transaction. Politics! My father, he wants to show The Hague that the French are our allies, and you know I need the money—"

"*Money?*" Maghfira thundered, starting to pace like a caged animal. She glared at him, willing Constantin's tousled brown hair to burst into flames. "You are abandoning me for money? You...heartless, selfish, inconsiderate beast!" She felt a sob building in her chest and choked it down, determined not to let him break her heart. You need *money*? She felt herself drifting away from the world. "Very well!" she continued in kind. "I wish you exactly what you are looking for. I will not trouble you any longer."

"Maggie, Maggie, wait!" Constantin moved to block her exit,

taking her by the elbows and bending to look her in the eye. "You did not read on. Please! I am not abandoning you, not now, not ever! Listen!" Maghfira turned her head, refusing to look at him. He continued. "Things will continue between us just as before." He took her chin between his fingers and tried to turn her back towards him. "I will be in Amsterdam for weeks, months even, no matter what my affairs in Paris become. It will call—for a little more discretion, is all. Maggie!" He pleaded. "I *love* you!"

She closed her eyes as she realized what he was proposing. He thought to keep her as a lover, forever waiting on his convenience. *A fake wife, too*, she thought. She pulled away, blinking away tears before he could see.

"Eelke would not let me in," she told him, realizing what that meant. "You will not let me return here."

"Maggie, please!" Constantin moved to her side, fixing her with a soft, fatherly look that meant he was going to treat her like a child. "I will come to you instead, at any hour—at all hours! You will have me in the comfort of your own bed. You must understand how foolish it would be to receive you here."

Almost as foolish as it would be for me to receive you there, Maghfira thought. She wanted to slap him, to scream obscenities, to repay him for the insult to her honour that he was so oblivious to. But she could not let him know her position, not now. She refused to be at anyone's mercy.

The tightness in her chest made her cough, bringing up the ash-flavoured residue of her losses with it. She waved away Constantin's move to help her and braced herself against the table, staring hard at the map of Eleusis. *I don't belong in Amsterdam any more than I belong on the moon*, she thought, tracing the city's curling paths with a dry finger.

"I will miss this place," she said truthfully, straightening. She turned back to Constantin and forced herself to smile. "I will have little enough to read."

"Darling." Constantin's eyes lit up. "You can borrow whatever you choose. You will be my dearest secret, the most beautiful escape. You shall have everything you want." He stepped forward and adjusted the spectacles that had fallen askew across her face. It took all Maghfira's will not to swat his hands away, to keep smiling like an imbecile instead.

"May I start with those?" she gestured at the moon. Constantin frowned.

"That's just nonsense, Maggie," he said, shutting the book and taking her hand. "Why not the new volume of Vondel? You adore poetry."

"Are you afraid you will never see your books again, my love?" she pouted, hanging back. Constantin hesitated, looking torn. "Won't you indulge me in my fancies? The volumes will always be waiting for you, after all, safe with me." She wore her sweetest smile, but her meaning was clear. She must have something of value, something to hold in trust, to ensure he will come and see her again.

Constantin said nothing for a moment, only glancing back and forth between Maghfira and the books. She could see guilt warring with apprehension, trust with fear. These books were valuable to him, just as the map had been to the VOC men, that was clear. *Nonsense, indeed! You know exactly what these are.* Maghfira could only pray that she was still just as valuable to him.

"Of course," he capitulated, false levity in his voice. "You know I can deny you nothing, darling."

Maghfira capitulated, too, agreeing to everything the man said and did. When his porter took her out the servants' entrance carrying for her six volumes of cosmography, she agreed to receive him at her home the following week, without mentioning it had been gutted by fire, or that she did not plan to be there.

Yes, you can have it all. The whole world. But not the moon.

***

She sold two of Constantin's books immediately, leaves and binding separately. Even on such short notice, they brought a handsome sum, enough to supply her with new equipment and a room in a hotel on the Herengracht canal.

She copied both maps of Eleusis—Janssonius' and the one from Constantin's library—from memory and propped them side-by-side on a windowsill. The VOC men had invaded her home in order to take this moon, and yet there it was, comfortably displayed in the Huygens library as if everybody knew of it. *They* already had a map of Eleusis. They simply didn't want her to have one too. They wanted to control this information, not destroy it. What for?

Proposition 6. Maghfira read, slowly limping through *A World in the Moon*, the first of the English books. *That there is a world in the Moon hath been the direct opinion of many ancient, with some modern, Mathematicians, and may probably be deduced from the tenets of others...*

She forced herself to think harder. Nobody was conducting a war on telescopes or burning down observatories. It was the maps that were contentious. They showed something the Earth-bound could not observe. She had stared at the moon often enough and seen nothing unusual. Why destroy fanciful pictures? Only the violent secrecy, and the corroboration of a second map, suggested to Maghfira that they showed something real. That Eleusis was real.

She glanced up at the side-by-side maps. The location of the city was identical, on the bottom-left corner of the dark side of the moon, trapped in a net of lines imagining a lunar longitude and latitude. The stars, too, were arranged in the same pattern. Some constellations were familiar to her, depicting a sky she remembered from her childhood. There was Crux, the first cross her father had taught her to wish by. Leo, Canis Minor, and Orion. And yet, if the constellations in this northern sky were different than those in the southern sky, shouldn't they be even more different when looking at the moon from the other side?

That isn't the moon's sky, she realized. *It's another map, laid out alongside the first.*

The mix of northern and southern constellations, the upside-down moon, even the hugeness of its surface were all hints. This was a map of the moon seen from a very specific place along the equator.

Eleusis can only be seen from the equator. That will be their point of departure. I need only reference the star charts. She continued to read the English book.

Proposition 13. So, perhaps, there may be some other means invented for a conveyance to the Moon, and though it may seem a terrible and impossible thing ever to pass through the vast spaces of the air, yet no question there would be some men who would venture this...

She recalled the business-like manner in which the bearded man had set her livelihood alight. The Dutch Republic was full of men who would, and did, brave vast oceans to barge into the worlds of others without knocking. Because of them, Amsterdam was the chief city in all the world, the richest and the keenest. Unobstructed by kings or popes, they would claim any corner of the Earth. Or beyond.

Of course they would not share Eleusis. The VOC had grown fat by refusing to share with anyone. Not the Spaniards, not the Portuguese, not the French. They wanted to keep the secret of a new land to themselves until they had it claimed and divided into shares. There was a city on the moon, and they were going to take it.

Two weeks later, Maghfira dressed all in black like any good VOC man. She prepared her portfolio and checked out of the hotel, unsure if she would ever be back. Then she set off for the East India House, headquarters of the VOC, where she meant to get the first true contract in a life dominated by facsimile.

***

The East India House was an edifice of ongoing construction, a muddy testament to wealth and progress. The brick facade marched unbroken down the Hoogstraat for blocks, guarding the VOC's secrets behind the unapproachable scale of the building, the biggest in Amsterdam. To the east lay the Kloveniersburgwal canal and the boats. Maghfira had arrived here six years ago, and the idea of leaving the same way felt in some way inevitable. She let herself in to the commons and made for the clerk's chambers.

"Mistress van Delsen," Bartelsz greeted her once the door had been shut behind her. "You have chosen an odd hour to visit."

"And yet you are working, Johan." Maghfira perched on the wobbly bench facing her broker's desk. The man shrugged.

"I am indeed. How can I help you, my lady? Are you ready, finally, to return to Batavia?"

Where I can find a rich husband and grow fat in the sun, like my mother? No, I don't belong there either. "I have another voyage in mind," she said, managing not to scowl. "I believe you have a ship headed for Nais."

"Nais?" Bartelsz said, his eyes widening in alarm. "You mean Sumatra, of course? I have a fluyt bound for Padang, but Nais, it's just a jungle. There's nothing there, my lady."

"I mean Nais," she said firmly, hoping she had read the star charts right. "I know there is a company expedition bound there, likely in October. If you know nothing of this, please take me to Governor-General Maetsuycker. I will put my request to him."

Bartelsz narrowed his eyes with suspicion. "Whatever you have heard of this expedition, my lady, you must have misunderstood. There is nothing for you in Nais."

"No. There isn't, is there? And yet, we will depart from that island, or somewhere near it." She locked eyes with him, hoping he recognized the same unwavering determination she'd had to undertake her first voyage. "I want to be added to the crew. I wish to be—" she sat straighter, testing the words, "— the cartographer."

Bartelsz balked. "Maggie, this is an audacious request, one I certainly cannot begin to—"

"I know what lies beyond Nais," she interrupted him, reconciling herself to stronger methods. "And if you know as well, you will take me to my lord Maetsuycker, or whoever has concerned themselves with that voyage, before I take my request to the Spanish." She tried to breathe normally, as if this were a simple request and not blackmail of the worst kind. Bartelsz's jaw quavered.

"Do not do this, Maggie," he begged, more disappointed than worried. "What could you possibly want—"

"Will you pass on my request, my lord?" She did not care to hear what derision he would lay on her. She already knew well enough where he thought she belonged—but he was wrong. She didn't belong anywhere.

Bartelsz sighed in resignation and nodded. He stood and beckoned her to follow him down the narrow stone halls, deeper than she could possibly dig herself out.

***

Bartelsz left her alone in the wide office of the Governor-

General. She stood, portfolio clutched in both hands, willing on herself the poise that said she believed absolutely that Joan Maetsuycker had no choice but to hire her.

The frown on Maetsuycker's face when he entered spoke its own stubborn story. The grey-haired man closed the door behind him and marched aggressively towards her, hands outstretched.

"Mistress," Maetsuycker barked, "show me your work." Maghfira nearly balked at the directness of his request, at his lack of manners. *How very like his underlings this man is.* She held out the portfolio to him, grateful that her arms did not shake.

He strode to his desk and unbuckled the leather case, flipping through the moon-maps and star charts within. Maetsuycker looked tired, then tore the top two pages out of their sleeve and tossed them unceremoniously into the fire.

"What!" Maghfira cried, furious.

"You are a great fool, my dear," he said. "And you have just made a madwoman of yourself. You will get out now. Thank you." He took two more pages, wadded them, and added these to the mounting flames.

"I will not!" she replied, stepping up to the desk and snatching one of her pages of notes. "I have come for Eleusis, and I will not go until you agree to add me to the voyage to Nais."

"My lady, you are in no position to make such demands. I know you. My men have been to your home and have destroyed everything in it. You have nothing to offer and nothing to threaten me with. You are a nuisance and that is all. You may go now while you still retain your dignity."

Maghfira's heart pounded as if she were about to leap from the pier. "You have destroyed nothing of me," she said, taking up a quill. "And you need me." She flipped the paper over and licked the quill before dabbing it in his inkpot. With a few quick, broad strokes, she traced again the outline of the moon and marked on it the location of Eleusis. She had begun to map out the stars when Maetsuycker snatched the sketch right out from under her. She stood straight, staring him down. His red-rimmed eyes looked at her as if she were some kind of abomination. "Burn it," she offered. "Burn them all. I will make them again. The map is in me and I know what it shows. You cannot undertake an expedition to a new land without a cartographer, so take me. You will find no one better."

"I could destroy you as easily as I have destroyed your scribblings, woman," he said, crumpling this last sketch and putting it aside. "*If* I thought you were a threat. But the Spaniards will only think you mad, the Portuguese madder. A fanciful picture will mean nothing to them."

"I know exactly where and when Eleusis can be seen," she said. "I will commission a ship to Nais myself if I need to. You will find I am quite determined, my lord Maetsuycker."

"What I see," he said, sitting at his desk as if the discussion were making him too weary to stand, "is a villain who would sell out her nation to—"

"If this is my nation," Maghfira barked, frustrated, "then let me serve. What kind of leader are you, who cannot see a good tool when one is presented to him? All I want is to be part of something new. Something where the boundaries are not yet set, the fortunes not yet cast. You will find no one better suited," she repeated.

"You have threatened the Dutch Republic with treason or worse," Maetsuycker pointed out. "And my men will not want a woman on their ship." He frowned in earnest. "Bad luck."

"Would you rather a wet rag represent you in Eleusis?" she countered. "And as for luck," she shrugged, "tell them different fates rule the skies than the seas." *Hopefully.* "My lord, I am not leaving."

The creases on Maetsuycker's forehead retreated in thought. Maghfira tracked his gaze to a framed print on his wall: the moon, as rendered by the artist van Langren. She wondered if she were to flip it over, if she'd find Eleusis hiding in the shadows beneath.

After a long moment of silence, he nodded. "Let us test your resolve then, my lady." He placed the remaining sketches from her portfolio on the fire and held up a hand. "You will not need them if you are as good as you say. Come."

Maghfira was determined not to let the Governor-General's fatalism scare her. The only thing she was absolutely sure of was her resolve. She followed him out the door and through the endless halls of the East India House, praying with every step that he was not leading her to a dungeon—or to an executioner. They finally came to a plain door with one lock, which he opened. Beyond it was darkness. Maghfira hesitated.

"The noose has been around your neck ever since you set foot in my domain, my lady," Maetsuycker said. "It is no more dangerous in there than anywhere. Has your courage run dry already?" Maghfira glared at him and stepped into the blackness.

The coolness of outdoor air hit her within a few steps. Moonlight bathed an interior courtyard strewn with unfamiliar constructions, the chief of which was an enormous cannon built at one end of the long yard. Maetsuycker lit a lantern and led her towards it. A contraption of shining gold sat tethered atop the long neck and caught the lamplight, shining like a beacon. Maghfira gawked.

"Our great hope for reaching Eleusis, or somewhere else up there," Maetsuycker waved at the waning moon above them.

He held the lantern high as they approached the cannon, illuminating the golden sphere's portholes and limp sails. It was no bigger than a covered carriage, but sealed as tight as a barrel. He turned to scrutinize her. "We have not yet tested it with men inside, but the unmanned flights have been promising. The greatest minds in the Dutch Republic have informed its construction, and it will take the bravest to pilot it. We are training the crew by locking them in vaults for hours at a time." He almost smiled then, taunting her again. "Cramped, without fresh air or light, occasionally jostled in the most violent manner. Who knows how long and how arduous the journey will be? We must prepare for the worst. Do you think you could do it, Mistress van Delsen? Ride the winds packed into a crate built by geniuses and lunatics, like a piece of stolen Antiquity? Some of our best captains have already quit the project. What makes you any better suited?"

"I have nowhere else to be," Maghfira said softly, still taking in the contraption's golden wheels and joints. "I don't belong here."

Maetsuycker's face softened. "Ambitious people seldom feel as if they belong, my lady. After all, who would venture into the unknown if they were content with what they already had?"

Maghfira stared at the golden vessel in awe. She imagined its sails unfurled, catching gusts from all directions, tenting first one way then another, tossing this little sun about the sky like a kite. Then she imagined gliding towards the Heavens in a moment of calm, the moon growing brighter at their approach. She imagined rolling to a stop on alien soil, unfolding herself in a new place. She imagined new oceans and new mountains, new roads and new buildings. She imagined the freedom of not being expected to belong.

"I could do it," she said.

FEASTING
HEATHER KAMINS

Heather Kamins is the author of a poetry chapbook,
Blueshifting (Upper Rubber Boot Books, 2011).
Her fiction and poetry have appeared in Pear Noir!,
Chiron Review, Neon, and elsewhere. She lives in
Western Massachusetts.

Maryellen Sterns was the first person I ever knew who died. I didn't even know her that well; she was in seventh grade and I was only in sixth. And yet a month after the car crash, she began appearing in my bedroom when I was trying to fall asleep. I didn't question why she chose me. It seemed impolite to ask.

I had never been a good sleeper, always dozing and rising, wandering around the house after my parents and brother were asleep. I flipped like a land-borne fish under the covers as sleep swallowed me up only to spit me out again. So I was used to the altered texture of the night: the odd creaks from phantom rooms, the warped squares of moonlight creeping across the walls. But I had never seen a ghost before.

She first appeared in my doorway deep into an early October night filled with lightning and thunder from a freak late-season storm. "Don't be scared," she said before I even saw her, and somehow, I wasn't. Dressed in jeans and a purple T-shirt I imagined she was wearing when the accident happened, she stayed where she was, waiting to be asked in. I had been trying to will myself to sleep by counting backwards from a million by sevens, and since that wasn't working, I saw no reason to turn her away.

She came over and sat at the foot of the bed. "Do you know Miss Lucy Had a Baby?" she asked.

I nodded, and we clapped our hands together and sang. Her

hands felt strange against mine: solid, yet not solid. Like they had mass, but no temperature.

Miss Lucy had a baby, she named him Tiny Tim, she threw him in the bathtub to see if he could swim.

The rhythm of our clapping was oddly soothing.

He drank up all the water, he ate up all the soap, he tried to eat the bathtub but it wouldn't go down his throat.

I fell into a sort of trance, going through the lines automatically and only regaining awareness of what I was doing when we reached the end.

Out went the doctor, out went the nurse, out went the lady with the alligator purse.

Maryellen put her hands in her lap and peered around my room, checking out my books and stuffed animals.

"What do you want to do now?" I asked.

"I dunno."

I was feeling constricted under the sheets, so I stood up and stretched. Maryellen came up next to me, alert and ready to follow me to our next activity. I couldn't think of anything else to do with her in my room that wouldn't be boring to her, so I wandered downstairs to the kitchen. I kept looking over my shoulder, expecting her to vanish between glances, yet she was there each time I checked.

I got myself a glass of water, drank half of it, and set the glass down on the counter. Maryellen stood next to it and waved her hand back and forth through it. "Can you feel that?" I asked.

She shook her head.

I was going to go into the living room, but Maryellen seemed stuck on the current situation. She poked one finger through the side of the glass and wiggled it around in the water. Not even a ripple on the surface. I strolled around the room a couple times and then opened the refrigerator. While it had been half empty that afternoon when I went to look for a snack, it was now filled to capacity with bowls and platters I had never seen before. "What's this?" I mumbled, pulling out a large plate shaped like a lotus flower and putting it on the counter next to the water glass. Maybe my mother was throwing a dinner party. But had she bought all new dishes?

Maryellen whipped her head toward the plate. "What is that?"

"I don't know," I said. I pulled a gossamer cloth napkin off of the plate's contents, which turned out to be a circle of small teacakes dusted in powdered sugar. Before I had time to consider whether or not to try one, Maryellen grabbed a cake and took a big bite. "Mmm!" she said, biting into it again.

"You can eat that?" I asked, skipping over the fact that her ghostly hands could pick it up in the first place.

She nodded, her mouth too full to speak.

Hesitant, I reached out and picked up a cake. It was lighter than I expected. I took a tiny nibble from the edge, and the flavors overwhelmed me. I didn't recognize them then, but many years later I tasted them again and remembered lavender, bergamot, a highly fragrant type of vanilla bean. "Whoa," I said between bites, lightheaded.

If the food were for a dinner party, I would get in serious trouble for eating it, yet I couldn't help myself. Maryellen and I finished off the cakes, and then I pulled out one dish after another after another, and we stuffed ourselves, half drunk on the scents and tastes of everything. Between a dish of golden sweet potato fritters with tamarind sauce and a bowl of cardamom spiced pudding, it occurred to me to ask her, "Do you usually eat?"

"Nope," she said. "This is the only food I can have now." She stuck her hand right into the pudding and scooped some into her mouth.

We sat on the floor bathed in refrigerator light and devoured every morsel of food on those dishes, savoring each bite. No daytime food I'd ever tried had tasted so sweet, so rich, so flavorful. I was so sated that I fell asleep right there on the tiles, the empty dishes piled all around us.

I woke to the sound of my mother coming down the stairs. It was light out, and Maryellen was gone. I jumped up off the floor to put away the platters and bowls before my mother saw them, but there were no dishes anywhere. Peeking into the refrigerator, I saw no sign of any unusual plates or fancy food.

"You're up early," my mother said, coming around the open fridge door to where I was standing.

"Have you seen that big plate that looks like a flower?" I asked without thinking.

She looked at me quizzically. "Which one?"

I held my hands about a foot apart. "This big. A big pink flower. Or purple, maybe?"

"We have those nice china plates with the yellow flowers on them. Is that what you're thinking of?"

"No," I said, more insistent. "The whole thing was shaped like one big flower."

She peered at me. "Hmm. I think maybe you're thinking of something else. Maybe something Grandma or Aunt Farrah has?"

I wanted to argue more, to push the point, but I could tell it would be useless. "Never mind."

"You want some breakfast?" my mother asked.

"I'm not hungry," I said, and went to get dressed for school.

***

Maryellen's car accident had happened one evening when

she was on the way home from soccer practice, just one week after school started for the year. Everyone at school found out the next morning, and we all sat around and talked all day instead of doing any classwork. The entire student body was shuffled into the auditorium so the guidance counselor and the principal could talk to us about the feelings we might be having, and then they released us back to our homerooms, where everybody gathered into pairs or little groups and talked about their experiences with Maryellen. "She gave me a piece of gum one time," said Stacy Lucas. "One time she said she liked my shoes," said Taneesha Blake. Lilly Pressley kept crying, and when she left the classroom to go to the bathroom, Jessica Saperstein rolled her eyes and said, "She's so fake. She barely even knew Maryellen."

I didn't say much of anything. Mostly, I watched everyone else reacting, wondering what it was I was supposed to be feeling. There was some emotion brewing deep down in my gut, someplace I couldn't access, but I didn't want to make the wrong impression as Lilly had. So I listened to everyone else, nodding and trying to look serious. Meanwhile, my mind rode through the narrower, twistier streets of town, the ones with barely enough room for two cars to pass each other, the ones with big, old trees right at the edge on either side. I pictured broken glass and splintered branches, and there was a hole the shape of a ghost in the center of my chest.

***

Maryellen came to my room again the night after she first arrived. This time, she didn't bother with niceties. She appeared by my bed, and as soon as I saw her, she said, "Let's go eat something."

Part of me felt hurt that she seemed more interested in the food than in me. But, I, too, wanted to feast again. I could still taste the flavors of spices and flowers on my tongue. "I don't even know if anything will be in there," I said, but she had already evaporated through the door. I got up and followed her downstairs. In the kitchen, she stood waiting for me to open the refrigerator. "Can't you just stick your hand through the door?" I asked.

"I can't see what's in there if the light's not on, and you have to open the door to turn on the light." Obviously.

I grasped the handle, and a nervous anticipation filled me. What if the feast had been only a one-time event? Would she leave if it had? "There might not be anything there," I said again, bracing myself for her sudden annoyed departure if the refrigerator turned out to be empty, but Maryellen waved my concerns away.

I cracked the door open, not even enough to switch on the light, and Maryellen said, "Come on!"

Finally, I took a deep breath and swung the door wide. The shelves were packed with brightly colored dishes, and Maryellen squealed with delight. As I let out a relieved giggle, an electricity tingled through me, and my mouth watered. I began pulling things out and setting them on the floor. Somehow, it seemed more appropriate to eat down there than at the table or the counter.

There was a deep cobalt blue bowl filled with a fruit salad of mangosteen and dragonfruit cut in the shape of intricate flowers and coated in just the right amount of a light honey syrup. There was a silver platter of spicy pork and black bean dumplings with a tangy, salty dipping sauce. There was a black and red lacquered box containing rich dark chocolates with fillings of rose petal cream and pistachio ganache. We dug in, we reached over each other to try everything, we squealed and moaned with delight as we tasted each new dish. We ate all of it.

The next morning, I woke to find that I had somehow

waddled up to my bed after feasting, again leaving the dishes strewn all over the floor. I went down and checked the kitchen, and once again, there wasn't any hint of the night's activities, not a plate, not a single crumb. I wasn't going to ask my mother about the mystery food this time, not after the conversation about the flower plate. And anyway, she would have brought it up if that much food had gone missing.

***

Each night for weeks, the ghost showed up in my room, and we went downstairs and stuffed ourselves on all the dazzling night foods, and each morning, there was no sign any of it had happened. I had no one to talk to about my new friend, and I wondered if, in fact, we were friends at all. With each feast, Maryellen grew less interested in talking to me and more interested in the food. I pretended it didn't bother me. After all, I couldn't stop thinking about those flavors, either. Sometimes I peeked during the day, but the food only showed up after dark. I began to grow tired, unable to focus in school. The other kids didn't talk to me, and I didn't talk to them. I felt irritable when the teacher called on me, and spent a lot of time daydreaming about passionfruit custard and chili paste, the mysteries of the midnight refrigerator. *What if it stops?* I worried. But the strange nocturnal banquets kept coming.

I felt heavy from all that eating, yet when I weighed myself on my parents' bathroom scale, I was the same as I had been at my checkup a month earlier. Maybe it was my soul that was heavier. I grew cranky with my family, and when my parents sat me down after dinner one night to talk about my recent behavior and see if something was wrong, I barely heard them. My eyes drifted past them to the refrigerator. Would the feasts still be in there even if I didn't open the door to find them? The Zen riddle of it whirred in my mind, my father's voice only background noise. I thought of ruby pomegranate seeds, the warm tones of saffron and turmeric, brightly colored dishes of beautiful food piled like jewels in a safe.

***

One chilly night in early December, I tucked myself into bed early, but I couldn't sleep at all. I listened as my brother went to bed, and then my parents, and then the house was quiet. I kept thinking about the refrigerator and the bright feast waiting for Maryellen and me. Where was she? What time was it, anyway? Wasn't she usually here by now? How could she keep me waiting like this? I fidgeted and glanced at the clock until I couldn't stand waiting any more, and then I went downstairs without her.

I counted out the stairs as I tiptoed down into the dark kitchen. With one hand on the refrigerator handle, I felt a clammy panic edging its way along my skin. What would I do if I only discovered the mundane contents that had been there that afternoon? Would Maryellen grow bored with me without all that food to eat? Had she already grown bored with me, and that was why she hadn't come?

But the feast was there, and it was even more bountiful than usual. I found myself eating before I even thought about it, and I couldn't stop. Oh, the flavors of cinnamon and basil, of olives and sumac, of honey. The food that night, eaten all by myself, was the most delicious of all the midnight feasts.

A small ceramic pot caught my eye. I took it out, removed the lid, dipped my index finger into the cool center, and tasted. It was a tangy lime curd. Just like Maryellen had done with the spiced pudding that first night, I plunged my hand into it and shoved it into my mouth as though I were starving.

"What are you doing?" said a voice from across the room. Maryellen. She had come after all, and now she stared at me, horrified, but I didn't stop. "Why didn't you wait for me?"

I didn't answer. I was ashamed, but I couldn't help myself. I licked the last of the lime curd out of the pot and grabbed an elaborately carved crystal bowl of meatballs from the top shelf of the refrigerator. Maryellen charged toward me, right through the kitchen island, and we struggled as she tried to grab my arm and spin me toward her so she could get at the dish. As she clutched at me, I felt that familiar not-quite-solid feeling of her hands pressing on me, like the way a heavy rain feels against the skin. She twisted and turned and reached into and through the bowl to try and grab a handful of meatballs. But I held the dish close, dodging and keeping my back to her, shoving meatballs into my mouth as fast as I could so I could have them all to myself. The flavors of oregano and lemon zest sang on my tongue.

"Give me that!" shouted Maryellen, coming around my side and grabbing the edge of the bowl. "It's supposed to be for me!"

"No!" I shouted.

"You get everything! You can have whatever you want during the day!"

"It's mine!" I screamed, turning away from her again, but I lost my balance and the dish slipped out of my hands and shattered on the floor, the meatballs rolling in all directions. "Look what you did!" I shrieked, diving to the floor to pick up the food. I couldn't bear to waste it. I grabbed at the meatballs, cutting my hands on the crystal shards as I flailed. All the while, I kept expecting Maryellen to push me away so she could get the food herself, but it was only me on the floor.

"I should go," Maryellen said from somewhere behind me.

"Wait," I said, but when I turned to look, she was already gone.

Though her leaving meant I didn't have to share, I felt uneasy when she disappeared, the same uneasiness I felt that day when we found out she had died. Something curdled in my stomach, and I slowly rose and went upstairs. I lay in bed for a long time, feeling haunted, and only began to doze when it started getting light outside.

In the morning, the food was again gone, but the scratches and cuts on my hands remained. I told my mother I was sick to my stomach and couldn't go to school. I spent most of the day sleeping, and when night came, I waited to see if Maryellen would come back. She didn't. Sometimes, on the many nights that followed, I woke up in the dark to the feeling of being watched, but I never saw her again. When I checked the refrigerator, I found only the normal leftovers and ingredients. I checked it every night for a while, and then less frequently, but the feasts never returned. Over time, I started sleeping better, and the heaviness inside me grew lighter. But even now, decades later, I still find myself up past midnight every once in a while, and I peek inside my own refrigerator. Even now, when I taste rose petals or cardamom, I shiver and look over my shoulder for the ghost of a girl.

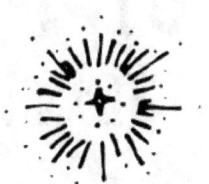

INGEBJORG UNSPELLED

JESSAMY DALTON

Jessamy Dalton lives in rural Virginia, where she reads, writes, pulls weeds on the family farm, and somehow keeps existing despite the fact that most of society considers neither writing nor farming 'real' jobs.

This story first appeared in Lorelei Signal, April 2011.

You probably won't believe me, but I knew Magister Klovass was going to be trouble the first moment I laid eyes on him. Yes, I have hindsight now, and yes, everyone knows how it turned out, and they can all tell you how inevitable it was, but I was the only one there at the beginning, and I remember. Mother called me into the solar and said, "Ingebjorg, darling, I want you to meet the most *wonderful* man," and there was this oily little fellow with lips like a fish. He made me a smarmy little reverence, and even as I was returning it with a curtsey, I thought to myself, *you're going to be a problem, aren't you?*

You might argue, as Mother did, that I only disliked Klovass because he wasn't the sort of man I was used to. Father, the king, is one of those blond, hearty men, with a high color from wining, dining, and riding, and a body you might describe as "running to fat" until you bump into him and realize that what you've been calling fat is solid muscle—and his courtiers are pretty much cut from the same mold, so no, I wasn't used to men who smelled of violet water and wore pointed slippers. But it was Klovass' manner, not his looks, that really struck the warning bell in my mind.

Or, if I must be honest, it was the way that Mother's manner changed after he came around.

My mother is a very intelligent woman. She can speak four languages, play three instruments, write poetry, calculate geometry, and discourse on philosophy, astronomy, and theology. Father always swells with pride when he lists her accomplishments. She's not the sort of woman you'd expect to find out here in the forests and fjords of the Northlands, and Father loves to brag on her to his fellow thanes. Father himself is smart enough, in his own sphere of things, but not exactly what you'd call intelligent. And I take after Father.

You know, it is strange how one person can like certain things in another person, as long as that person is of the opposite sex; but put those traits in a person of the same sex, and the first person can't stand it. What I mean is, Mother adores Father. Absolutely adores him. Maybe he isn't her intellectual equal, and maybe they don't have many interests in common, but he is the only person who can make her laugh—I mean really laugh, not tee-hee-titter at something clever—and he is the only person who can get through to her when she's in one of her fits. "Now, Frideswiede," he'll say, "what is this nonsense? You are stirring yourself up for no reason. Calm down!" And she will. But if *I* tried taking that tone with her...? Let us just say that Mother and I have always been fonder of each other the farther apart we are.

But there are many things I understand better now, after what happened, and I've come to realize that my mother, under all her sophistication, has always felt very unloved and alone. So when she found my father, it was wonderful—until she became afraid that someone would take him away. She could convince herself of her superiority over any other woman—who could match her for wit and charm?—but then I came along. Father's daughter, his apple, his little bird, his heart. And I grew up to look like him, blond and big (in the right places, anyway), and I grew up to sound like him, act like him, ride, hunt, and feast like him. And while I grew up, Mother grew older.

She would sit with us at supper, a wimple over her greying hair, and listen while Father and I talked about horses and dogs and how funny it was when Nils the Hawk-Master split his pants, and she would grow cold. I did not see it, and neither did Father, how fears of age and loss, and doubts of herself and of love, were festering in her finely-strung mind, until the littlest things—a new bauble Father got me, the plums I left on his night-stand—became invested with dark and terrible meanings. We did not see it, but Klovass did.

He claimed to be a professor of alchemy. This was a new pursuit of my mother's, alchemy. Klovass came with an introduction from one of Mother's learned friends, and a promise to teach her the secrets of transmuting base metals into noble substances. But his true talent was the ability to transform other people's weaknesses into advantages for him. Like an eel (which, come to think, he resembled), he wriggled his way into Mother's confidence. Seizing upon her deepest fears, he fanned up a raging bonfire in her mind, the pain of which only he could ameliorate.

Someone who has just peered over my shoulder and claims some superior knowledge says that I should not be mixing my metaphors—having begun with an eely comparison, I should continue in an aquatic vein, and not go dodging off into talk of bonfires. To which I reply that my mother is the poet, not I, and I am only recounting how it seemed to me: Klovass slinking around in satin, berating the servants as if they were his own, while Mother sat restless day and night, scarcely able to pass an hour without the Magister's reassurance. Of course I tried to get Father to do something. But he thought it was good that Mother had an educated person to keep her company, and he couldn't imagine any danger from a man who didn't even know a goshawk from a falcon.

This uncomfortable state of things persisted for about two months, until the day I returned from an outing to find Mother waiting for me in the Hall. She asked me where Father was. I replied that we had been out riding together, and now he was in his bath. With a bitter laugh, she asked me what he thought he needed cleansing from.

"Oh," I said, "everyone feels like a bath these days, there is such a stench around the place—perhaps it is all those alchemical experiments." Mother rounded on me, teeth bared, nose white. I waited for her to start shrieking and throwing things, as she usually did, but she only muttered some strange syllables under her breath.

I said, "What?" and she repeated herself in a raised voice, but the words still did not make sense. She giggled at my confusion.

"Do you know what that was?" she said. "That was the Binding of the Fate from the Mystic Q'bala." She walked idly around the room as she spoke, running her hand over random objects. "The Binding of the Fate ties a person to a certain destiny—a destiny she cannot escape, no matter how hard she tries. Every action she takes to avoid it leads her back into its heart. Every resistance mires her deeper. It is like a spider's web: delicate, elegant—deadly."

"Indeed," I said, keeping my voice as dry as possible. "May I ask what fate have I been, as you claim, bound to?"

Mother's eyes were dark and glittery, their natural blue drowned behind dilated pupils. *"You will cause the destruction of this house by fire. You will cause the death of your father. You will wed a man of foul description, and he will be your master for the rest of your life."*

I tried to laugh, but it stuck in my throat. I could only stare. When I was nine, I'd had a cat, a sweet, affectionate tabby that slept on my bed and shared my morning milk-porridge. But once I'd come upon it in the grass, killing a baby bird, and its face at that moment had been unrecognizable to me, sharper and cruel, primeval. I thought of this now, as I looked at my mother. I took a step backward, and then another. She found the laugh I had lost, and it echoed behind me as I fled.

I went where I always went when I was upset: the stables. Hidden in the straw in my favorite hunter's box, with my head resting on his flank, I made an attempt to think rationally. But too many pictures were running through my mind: my elbow, knocking over the candle on my dressing table, the hangings going up in flame...a coal, swept by my skirts from the hearth into the room, catching the rushes on the floor...Father and I out hunting, my crossbow discharging by accident, the quarrel lodging in his throat...Father, eating a pear I'd given him and choking...Father, reaching to catch a ball I'd thrown, and slipping, falling, striking his head on a rock...

(The same critic has just looked over my shoulder again and asked me why I had no terrible visions of the foul man I was fated to marry. I tell him to be quiet.)

I stayed in the stables until dark. By then I had decided to leave. Despite Mother's assertions that nothing could change my fate, I had to do something, and going away, quickly and quietly, seemed best. I crept into the stablehands' quarters, took a suit of boy's clothes for disguise, and gathered food and such sundries as I thought I might need. I was ruthlessly practical, and proud of myself for it. I didn't even start to blubber when I said good-bye to the dogs. I simply patted them on the head, laced my boots, and struck out into the night.

The journey was strange. The forest, my old familiar hunting ground, felt different in the dark: ancient, stern, and remote. The boughs of the firs hung over me, silent and watchful, offering no harm, but no help, either. I was a mere flesh-creature, squashy and short-lived. The trees had seen many of my kind come and go, and were not interested in my problems. Nothing seemed real. My body moved along competently enough, but it did not feel like it belonged to me. I tried to keep the wind on my face, but I still lost all sense of direction. I have no memory of sitting down to rest, but I must have, for suddenly, the birds were singing, the sun was peering down, and an old woman was tending something over a fire nearby.

I sat up and squinted at her. She had a face like an old potato and was wearing so many skirts and shawls it was impossible to determine her actual shape. Seeing me awake, she grinned, revealing two lone teeth, and handed me a clay cup.

"Get that inside you, your Lady Highness Princess Ingebjorg, and you'll feel better," she said.

"Thank you, Old Mother," I replied, having been taught to be gracious to the common people, and then, spoiling the effect somewhat, blurted out, "How did you know me?"

"I'm your godmother, lovey," she said.

I started to say, "No you're not, my godmother is the wife of the Thane of Rjinswold, I know because she sends me little presents on my name day, like a silver sewing kit, or a book of morally uplifting essays," but I stopped. That was my official godmother. This was my other one.

You see, the character of the heir to a kingdom is very important to that kingdom's subjects, so whenever a royal baby is born, the wisest men and women from every village get together and choose one of their number to be the child's unofficial guardian. This godparent watches over the prince or princess as they grow, sometimes arranging for a lesson to be learned, sometimes smoothing the path of true love, sometimes just remaining close to hand in case the royal youngster runs into the sort of problem that stumps all the king's horses and his men too.

Like this one.

I drained the contents of the cup (it was a ferny-tasting tea), and poured out my story to the old woman. She was a good listener. When I was done, she sat with her thumb on her chin, thinking. Then she said, "You've got a twig in your hair, lovey, right about there." Then she thought some more. Finally she said, "Well, I don't know much about mystic kwabalers and such, but I do know this: the thing to ward off evil is good, and the way to break a curse is to fulfill it."

Panic filled me in spite of myself, and I squawked, "*No—!*" but the old woman just patted my hand. "Trust me, lovey," she said. "I won't let it go bad." Then she hoisted herself to her feet and trotted off at a surprising speed, leaving me no choice but to follow. We soon came to a rough track, where a woodcutter with a bullock-cart just happened to be passing. Godmother inveigled us a ride with shameless claims of sore feet and old bones, and we arrived back at the castle so quickly I could only conclude that either I'd been walking in circles all night, or the old woman had some magic in her.

She left me in the cart while she popped into the kitchens to see how things lay. Returning, she reported that the King (that is, Father) was out hunting with his courtiers, and Mother and her pet alchemist were off on some mystical errand, gathering newt's eyes, no doubt. My pain must have shown on my face, because Godmother patted my hand again. "Be strong now, lovey, for I'm going to need your help. I can't give orders to your people here, but you can. This is what we're going to do…"

A few minutes later, I strode into the Hall and asked the seneschal to call all the servants, from the Head of Cellars to the lowest scullery maid. When they were assembled, I cleared my throat, and, in as haughty a voice as I could manage, explained what I needed them to do. There were many blank stares, and more than a few significant tappings of fingers on foreheads, but I was obeyed. Every able-bodied person in the household immediately began to gather up our earthly goods and carry them outside into the fields.

Beds, tables, chairs, tapestries, chests, pots, pans, spoons, feather pillows, eiderdowns, greaves, cuirasses, daggers, the stag's head from the hall…combs, mirrors, razors, heaps of linen, boots, shoes, a game of draughts, a pair of silver dice… bowls, goblets, the iron strongbox from Father's room, spinning wheels, looms, a birdcage, a lute…when it was all piled on the ground, I thanked the puffing servants graciously and gave them the rest of the day off. They wasted no time scuttling down to the village, where it would soon be common news that the Princess Ingebjorg had gone completely bonkers. I walked through the now-echoing rooms with my godmother.

"Are you sure this will work?" I asked her.

"Nearly," she said, taking a nip of the wine that we were sprinkling liberally around the floor.

The castle made a beautiful blaze. Flames leapt out windows, roof tiles popped and shattered, beams collapsed in showers of embers, everything. Godmother and I admired the show from a safe distance, finishing up the wine and swatting out stray sparks. I was just congratulating myself on an easy job when a humanoid creature came charging out of the woods and began to fling dirt on the flames in a frenzied way. "I can get them out! I must get them out!" it was crying. Godmother and I ran to restrain it, or him (for close to it, it was obvious that under an amazing collection of rags and dirt the creature was a young man, not many years older than myself). Finally, we impressed on him that everyone was safe.

Instead of being relieved at this news, the strange boy seemed to fall into despair. "I thought it was my chance to break the curse," he moaned, slumping to the ashy ground. Godmother offered him a drink. My ears had pricked at the word curse.

"You are under some sort of enchantment, sir?" I asked, kneeling beside him.

He snorted and flung out his arms. "Am I under—just look at me!"

I looked. He flushed and fidgeted.

"I used to be a prince," he said, more quietly. "When I was barely out of boyhood, a great magician came to our court and won my father's confidence. He soon convinced my father that I was worthless and a shame to him, and the two of them drove me out with nothing but the clothes on my back. I will be allowed to return only when I have won my fortune. And I have tried, you know, but the wealthy won't let me near them because I'm dirty and I smell, the poor are suspicious of me because my manners are too fine, the knights say I'm too thin to be a fighting man, and the beggars say I'm too stout to beg. So I've been living alone in the forest, growing more wretched by the day."

"This magician," I said. "Was he a greasy little man with knock-knees and a laugh like *a-heh-heh*?"

"No," said the prince. "He was a tall bony man with black fingernails and a chronic sniff like *snerrk*."

"Hmm," I said. "They must have studied at the same university."

But the prince was gazing at me with a rapturous look on the visible portions of his face. "Do you know you are the most beautiful thing I have seen in many months?" he murmured. I looked over at Godmother.

"Could do worse," she shrugged.

"Listen," I said to the prince, "there *is* something you can do—"

But before I could finish, the air was filled with the thundering of hooves. From the north, riding pell-mell, came the courtiers, Father at their head, his eyes wild and streaming. From the west came the carriage, Mother and Klovass tumbling out of it before it had fully stopped. My first instinct was to run to Father and throw my arms around his waist. But I refrained. I mustered as much dignity as one can whilst standing among piles of underclothing and mismatched spoons, and said, "My dear parents. No one regrets more than I the loss of my childhood home. But as you can see, all our goods have been protected, and our people are safe. That such a drastic measure should be necessary I also regret, but evil can only be overcome by good, and a curse can only be broken by fulfill—"

I thought I was doing quite well, but my pretty speech was drowned in a hubbub, as the courtiers battled small pockets of flame with far more energy than was necessary, and the servants poured back from the village, attracted by the smoke. Father approached me, but stopped short. His face was a mask of bewilderment. I could not meet his eyes. Godmother popped up behind him and tugged on his elbow, and he bent down politely so she could whisper in his ear. After a minute, he straightened up.

"Let me see," he said. "Ingebjorg was placed under a spell that she would cause the castle to be destroyed by fire, so to break this spell, she deliberately set the place on fire, only making sure that everything was safe beforehand. Is that right?" I managed a nod. "Ach, daughter," he said, running a stained hand over his face. "Sometimes you slay me."

I felt my heart break and mend, all in one instant.

"But what I don't understand," Father went on, "what I don't understand is, who would put a spell on Ingebjorg?" Godmother cackled and gestured towards Magister Klovass.

But he wasn't there. There was only the coach, rattling and swaying down the road as fast as it could go. Father roared. The courtiers scrambled for their horses and went in pursuit with wild whoops. As their dust cleared, I caught sight of Mother, standing white and rigid beside the charred remains of the Hall. Our eyes met across the ashes for a long moment. Then I turned away and took the prince's hand. "How about a bath?" I said.

So we ended up building two castles to replace the one that burned. Father and Mother live in the small tower by the forest, and Erik and I have a large, airy manor by the lake. Erik turned out to be quite handsome once he washed and shaved; Godmother was rather tiresome about it, and I had to be stern with her before she'd stop leering and winking every time she saw the two of us together. Father heaped all sorts of titles and honors on Erik, and we scared the wits out of his father by sending a procession of twelve royal carriages to invite him to the wedding.

Mother seems happier now that she has Father to herself. She's forsaken alchemy completely and taken up botany. Klovass was never caught, but Father issued numerous edicts forbidding him to so much as sneeze within the bounds of the kingdom. But my critic has piped up again, saying that I do not need to explain all this, that I can conclude my story by simply writing the words, *And they all lived happily ever after*, and that I ought to listen to him, because he is fated to be my master for the rest of our lives. But I tell him I have ways of breaking that part of the spell, too, and after a lengthy demonstration, he has to agree.

LARVAE
KAT TADDEI

Kat is a writer based out of Victoria, British Columbia.
She is in her fourth year of the Creative Writing program
at the University of Victoria, where she specializes in
fiction and drama.

The house is crying.

You try to calm it down, but nothing seems to help. Not singing, not scrubbing, not even spreading out your house-plants so that one sits in each of its windows like a candle. At night, the wood gasps softly, incessantly, and the heaters crackle as though the flames inside them are fighting to burst free. In her bedroom, the window is stuck halfway open; no matter how hard you pull it will not close, and so a chill floats from room to room, touching everything. But the ground-floor bathroom, the ground-floor bathroom is worst of all. Don't go in. Don't even walk past for fear of seeing it all over, hearing it all over, a tap running, the damp of wet floorboards, the stillness of bathwater unbroken by bubbles. No. No, squat outside when the need comes (although be careful to stay to the side of the house, away from the backyard). Later, lie in bed and watch the slanted ceiling walls creep forward with each breath you take. If you fall asleep, they'll come. Fat and writhing, they'll force their way into your nose, mouth, ears, digest you from inside until your hands are their hands and your face is their face and your body is nothing more than a breeding ground. Do not fall asleep.

The house is crying, and you can't fix it.

***

It takes fourty-eights hours to run out of Count Chocula, a

week to finish off Mrs. Morrison's ham-and-corn chowder, and fourteen days to empty the vegetable drawer of its last bell pepper, which you eat like an apple, even the core, until the tiny seeds wedged between your teeth are all the food left in the house. There's still lunchtime at school—mostly-hollow microwave quesadillas, frozen peas—so at least you won't starve too quickly. Try to go about your chores like usual. Laundry: the washer gurgles, then dies. Kick it a few times; nothing happens. Dishes: there haven't been any since you burnt the last of the pasta three days ago. Houseplants: how much water is too much, again? Pour in a little extra, just in case. Then a little more... a little more... Eventually the soil turns a deep, dark brown and water begins to overflow the pot. Stop.

It's day nineteen—a Sunday—when you finally admit the school's plastic-cheese sandwiches and canned peaches can't sustain you. Measures must be taken. Stand in front of the kitchen mirror at three a.m. and comb your long, black hair into two slick braids. *Wednesday*, the other kids used to call you, Wednesday Addams, with your sickly pale skin and eyes like eclipses. Your eyes are huge. Freakishly huge. It's three a.m. and your breath fills the whole house, from the icy tile under your bare feet to the rafters far above. Measures must be taken. Rub your fingers into a palette of halloween facepaint, smear black across your lips, and smile wide at your reflection in the mirror. There's a smudge of black on your front tooth; it tastes like chemicals.

Wednesday Wednesday, they used to chant, *who you gonna kill today?*

***

Outside, the streets feel noisy, despite the fact that there's no one around, only the odd taxi-cab which speeds by too fast to see if anyone's driving it. No, it's not a human noise you hear.

It's the streetlamps. They're humming to themselves, a high-pitched hum that raises hairs on your neck. The streetlamps, and the telephone wires, and the security alarms which blink like a row of little red eyes from above each and every doorstep—they're all humming. Wander down the middle of the deserted road, canvas bag in one hand, black slippers in the other. You had thought it would be too cold out to go barefoot on the cement, but the ground is strangely warm as you wade through puddles of orangey light (that, or your feet are numb).

Maple Park Grocery is a ten-minute walk, the only convenience store in your crummy edge-of-town neighbourhood. Its neon-red closed sign hums, too. The shop has been gated for the night, tall black bars encasing the "fruit & flowers" display out front. Poor flowers. The shop's weak fluorescent lights do nothing to help them grow, just like the last of the white bread did nothing to fill you up. Creep nearer. The bars aren't very close together, not for you anyway—but then you've never had a hard time slipping through cracks. You were such an underweight baby you once slid out of your cradle.

Toss your slippers through the gate and then follow their lead. Your chin and bum graze the metal, but the rest of your body squeezes through easy. It's a little claustrophobic, being on the other side, the world beyond now neatly sectioned off by the bars, but ignore your unease. Measures must be taken. Hum along with the neon closed sign as you pick through boxes of yesterday's produce. In the morning—the later morning—Mr. Ling will have his staff do just this, toss withered cabbage and bruised tomatoes to make room for fresh produce. No, no, you must not let him be wasteful. Bag a handful of browning mandarin oranges like shrunken jack-o-lantern heads, three overripe pears, a bunch of spotted bananas, and as many dates as you can fit in the pockets of your dress, minus two or three for a quick snack.

You're about to sneak back through the bars, the canvas bag now heavy against your waist, when you see it, tucked behind an obnoxious fuchsia bouquet. It's a small plant, its pot no wider than the palm of your hand, with silver leaves that curve bashfully into themselves. There's something almost elvish about it, something... what? Magical? No, not that. Something hidden, some secret tucked under those curling leaves, something which causes it to glow ever-so-slightly, even under dim fluorescents. Well, the house is down two plants from last week; for some reason, you can't help but zone out while watering them, and by the time your brain starts to whirr again, it's too late. But this one can be different. This one, you'll care for perfectly. Scoop it under your free arm; its leaves dance.

On your walk home, the moon decides to reveal herself, huge and naked and scarred. Pause in the middle of the street and howl at her, a single, unbroken cry, tender and tremulous and desperate as the final chord in a nocturne, a cry you didn't even know you'd been holding in. When you look to the sky next, she's gone, and it's started to rain.

***

It's four a.m. when you get home, bounty hugged under your arms. Of course, "bounty" makes it sound like you're a thief, which you're not. A thief? No. Can people even steal life? Because isn't that what it is, this houseplant, with its little moth-shaped leaves? A life? (Well, actually, it's a... a "silver maidenhair," according to the label.)

Abandon your groceries in the kitchen and take the stairs to your bedroom two at a time, black skirt swishing at your ankles, plastic pot hugged to your chest. No, not stealing at all. Your bedroom door is open a crack; nudge it with a bare toe and squeeze inside. Thankfully, other than the door (excitable thing), your room is just as it should be—encyclopedias nestled on their shelves, sheets tucked into their pillows, plants prim on the long, thin ledge by the bed.

Tiptoe to this ledge and crouch on the balls of your feet. Outside, the weather has gone from a soft pitter-patter to steady rainfall. An in-between rain. Start to resettle the maidenhair, move it from this dinky plastic thing to a solid clay pot. It's a young plant, all fresh and darkness free, and as you pat down the damp dirt of its new home, you are comforted by the—the—the what? The *rightness* of the act. Bury one thing, plant another.

It's this thought—bury one thing, plant another—which births a question in you. Lean in closer to the maidenhair, close enough to see each teensy vein on its pinky-sized leaves. Could it be—? It's timid like her, no doubt, not one leaf brushing against another, and modest too; you had hardly noticed it in the grocer's display, all hidden as it was by the fuchsia bouquet. But is it resilient? Quietly stubborn? Is it beautiful enough?

Pluck the freshly potted maidenhair from its spot on your bedroom carpet and make room for it in the centre of the window ledge. The moon remains half-hidden behind a veil of clouds, save for a few weak streams of light which pool on your window ledge before spilling across the carpet. The maidenhair's leaves glow silvery under the moon's touch, but it does not flaunt its beauty (unlike the big fern on the back porch, who is always stretching and preening and stealing sunlight from the smaller plants on either side of it). The feeling in your chest grows.

Of course, the maidenhair can't be *wholly* her. No reincarnated thing is every wholly the same. It cannot speak in a singsong voice, nor cup your face in slender, calloused hands. It does not know her stories of stalwart witches and lonely pixies, nor does it share her love for sugar cubes, nor the x-marks-the-spot scar on her chin. But none of that matters.

Crawl towards the plant on all fours, then gently, ever so gently, like the old rocking horse from those half-forgotten memories full of rightness and warmth, sway forwards and press your lips against its cool skin—not cold, or chilled, but *cool*. Close your eyes. Do you feel it?

Three thoughts come to you, three wonderful thoughts packaged tightly together, as though sent by the three moirai. One: this is what you have been waiting for, what *she* was *preparing* you for, all these years of tending her (now your) plants have been in anticipation of this moment. Two: the wrongness is gone—there is no rot in her leaves, no parasites chewing at her roots; she is happy. Three: you are no longer alone.

Overjoyed, you laugh and twirl about your bedroom, long black skirt swelling around you like an umbrella caught in the wind, twirl and twirl and twirl. You feel endless as a shooting star, endless and pretty and full of luck. But not luck, no—indeed, this is the unluckiest of occasions, un-lucky in the proper sense of the word: this is fate, a gift from atropos. Come to a dizzying halt and collapse, laughter still bubbling in your chest.

Not alone.

***

The next morning, you stand in front of the kitchen mirror, wiping your glasses with a hand towel until you've eliminated every last eyelash, dust particle and dried tear from the lenses. She watches patiently from the sink, next to a bar of lemon soap. It isn't until you've braided your hair and brushed your teeth (twice) that you catch on to how thirsty she is. Her leaves have such a slight droop to them that her need is barely noticeable, but you've learned to watch for signs like these—she was never any good at asking for help. Cup your hands under the sink's running water and pour a few palm-fulls into her pot. She perks up instantly.

On the bus ride to school, a girl with yellow pigtails and pumped-up pink sneakers tries to sit next to you and almost crushes her. Stupid, stupid girl! Doesn't she see this seat is occupied? Tilt your head downwards and glare at the girl past the arch of your forehead. *Wednesday, Wednesday, who you gonna kill today?* The girl calls you a word that doesn't matter in the slightest and spends the rest of the bus ride standing. Giggle when the bus comes to an abrupt halt and she flies forward, the rubber of her sneakers squeaking. Next to you, she sits dainty as a dove, leaves flinching only when the bus goes over a speedbump. How nice, to have someone to share the long ride with! Swing your legs and hum along with the bus for the rest of the ride, dum dee da.

In A block—math with Mrs. Dalhousie—sit in the back corner of the classroom running dirt through your fingers, as though it were still her russet hair. A fat pink robin perches on a branch outside the classroom window, stares in at you with little stone eyes. In its beak wriggles a half-eaten worm, wriggles even though its face, or rear, you can't tell, even though one of its ends is nothing more than a bloodied hole and its life is worthless anyway, wriggles and wriggles until finally the robin opens its beak and—

"Aislinn," Mrs. Dalhousie snaps, "are you practicing your long division?"

"Yes, Mrs. Dalhousie."

"No, you're not. I have eyes, you know. Now put that plant away and get to it. This is math, for goodness sake, not recess..."

 Curl the long, dark rope of your hair into a noose, curl it over and over. Mrs. Dalhousie used to be nice. She used to cook creamy pasta with a side of fresh-baked garlic bread whenever you had play-dates with her daughter. Used to top it off with a big bowl of lime green sorbet. But people can't be trusted, oh no. Nobody can ever be trusted to stay the same.

On your desk, she basks in a pool of sunlight, oblivious to Mrs. Dalhousie's rudeness. Her leaves coil upwards, smiling, comforting, as if to say, *I'm here, aren't I?* She looks so healthy, so full of life, it makes you smile, too. Of course. Nobody can ever be trusted to stay the same, but sometimes, that's for the better.

***

On your way out of class—you're always the last one to leave, taking special care to fold each textbook and binder into their proper place in your bag—Mrs. Dalhousie blocks the doorway.

"Aislinn, wait. Could we speak for a moment, please?"

She's clutching her Math 8 textbook to her chest and peering at you down her long, straight nose. But there's genuine worry in her grey eyes, the crease between her brows, so you shrug.

"Sure. For a moment."

She loosens her grip on the textbook. Her fingernails are painted bright pomegranate red, yet clipped tight to the nail-plate. Watch the way she shuffles across the classroom in her pointed brown loafers, then shuffles back, dragging a chair with her. It screeches against the hardwood—a bad noise, a painful noise, not just for you but for the poor chair, the poor floor, being ground together like two pieces of chalk. Mrs. Dalhousie steers the chair across from her desk, beckons for you to sit.

"Aislinn, I…" She drums her pomegranate nails against the textbook's cover. "I want to say I'm sorry. I shouldn't have snapped at you like that, earlier."

She blinks at you. Once. Twice. Then three, four, five times. People blink more the more uncomfortable they get. Hold her gaze.

"Aislinn? Do you accept my apology?"

"If you'd like me to." Make the mean woman squirm. Make her squirm like the half-eaten worm in the robin's beak. It doesn't work; instead, she sighs, rests her elbows against the desk.

"I don't know how else to bring this up. You've been... absent, lately? Not *physically*, that is, but... you've been elsewhere. During class. Not paying attention." Mrs. Dalhousie cocks her head at you, as if to ask if you're even paying attention now. "Aislinn, your grades are suffering. For goodness' sake, the past few days you've come to school dressed in Halloween costumes. Do you need to talk to someone? Maybe Ms. Melbourne?"

"I do not wear Halloween costumes," you say, indignant. "These are my clothes."

"Sweetie, you're wearing a witch's hat."

"Other kids wear hats to school. You don't say anything about them."

"Other kids wear toques, and beanies, and, and, and gangster caps. Although between you and me, I wouldn't mind if those were banned." Mrs. Dalhousie pauses, licks her pursed lips. "Aislinn, I hate to ask this, but... how is your mother doing? Is she back at the hospital yet?"

"She quit."

"Really?" Mrs. Dalhousie sits up straighter in her seat. "Well, has she... I mean... how are you two..."

"She's moved on."

"Well. That's... well. I hope that she's happier at her new job?"

"She's happier."

Mrs. Dalhousie's shoulders and forehead relax. "Then she'll be coming to parent-teacher interviews next week? I called your home, but the phone just rang and rang... Well, who can blame her? Sometimes all I want is to rip the damn thing off the wall, too."

Parent-teacher interviews? Hmmm. You weren't expecting that. Peer down at your lap, where she sits, her small wing-like leaves perky, attentive. She's almost shivering with excitement. Well, why not, then? It's not like parents are expected to say anything during these interviews. Just sit and absorb. And she's only gotten better at those two things lately.

"She'll be there," you say.

"Wonderful. Wonderful!" Mrs. Dalhousie is so excited she actually claps her hands together, although not with enough force to make any noise. "I have an open slot at 3:45. Will you ask her if that works?"

"It does."

⁂

"Burying another cat, dear?"

Jump at the sound of Mrs. Morrison's croaky, old-person voice. She's peering over the fence that divides your properties, though she's so peculiarly short that only the upper-half of her face is visible: a cloud of translucent white hair, an untamed unibrow, and two watery, bloodshot eyes. Mrs. Morrison is your sole neighbour, at least so long as the property at the end of the street remains abandoned, so perhaps she feels some kind of responsibility for you— that, or she's lonely. As far as you know, she's childless and husbandless, which would explain why nobody's come to collect her yet. A wild tomato plant has taken control of her back porch, its vines strangling the old house's already-shaky wooden beams, and in the summertime the whole yard smells of rotting fruit.

"Chestnut died two years ago," you say, "we haven't had another cat since."

"Ooooh. Right. Right." When Mrs. Morrison bobs her head, even the upper half of her face disappears beyond the fence. "What are you doing, then? Shouldn't you be in school?"

Drop the spade you've been working with and slap dry earth from your hands. You stole another plant last night, who knows why, a pot of star-shaped blue hydrangea. You tried arranging the hydrangea around the house, but it simply wasn't happy. It wanted to be outside, where it could see all its sister and brother stars high above, dangling around their elusive mother. Read the care instructions on the hydrangea's label as you answer Mrs Morrison. *When you plant your hydrangea, take care to give it lots of water, so it can establish its root networks.*

"It's Saturday."

"Saturday," Mrs. Morrison echoes you.

Make sure your hydrangea is planted in rich, moist soil, with plenty of nutrients for it to draw from.

"Say Aislinn, I haven't seen your mother lately. Is she still working at that hostel over there?"

Water deeply once a week. Do not be afraid of overwatering. Hydrangeas must be drowned in order to thrive.

"Aislinn?"

"What?" you snap.

"Is your mother still working at that hostel over there?"

"Hospital. Hospital, Mrs. Morrison, not hostel."

"Well, either way, I haven't seen her. Is she well?"

Snap your neck around to look at her. Her gross, vein-infested eyes are practically bulging out of her equally vein-infested head. Pick up the spade.

"She's fine."

"I wouldn't mind having a cup of tea with her one of these

days," Mrs. Morrison says, tone abject; you can practically see the quiver in her lip. "Did she like the ham and corn chowder?"

"Mrs. Morrison?"

"Yes, dear?"

Creep towards the fence. The wet grass squelches between your toes.

"If you don't leave, I'll kill you."

"What was that, dear?"

Grit your teeth and shift restlessly from foot to foot, spade clutched to your chest. "Leave. Or. Die."

Mrs. Morrison blinks. Once. Twice. Then three, four, five times.

"My, aren't you a little drama queen. Well, tell your mother I'm expecting her call."

Wait till Mrs. Morrison has inched her way across her lawn, up the back porch, and into the house before you look back at the instructions now crumpled in your fist.

Keep in mind, however, that your hydrangea will not last forever. If cared for and happy, however, it will bloom for a full season; so enjoy its beauty while it lasts!

***

"No, it's not a joke."

Mrs. Dalhousie's eyes are so wide you begin to imagine them outside of her body, two floating balls of goo staring at you. Why must she stare?

"Aislinn." Her voice is strained, and now you imagine the muscles of her throat on their own, too, thin strips of red stretched taught in the air beside her. She stands, paces in front of the chalkboard. "Where is your mother?"

"Right there." Fight to keep the irritation from your voice. She sits prim on the desk between you. In a week, she's grown to twice her original size. The brown stuff must taste good, despite its smell. She eats it up so quick, you considered having some yourself.

"Did you forget to tell her about the interviews? That's fine, Aislinn. Not a problem. But please, jus...stop. Stop this prank."

"I told you, *it's not a prank*."

"I thought it was for some kind of science fair," Mrs. Dalhousie mutters, "always carrying it around..."

"If you don't want to talk to her, can we leave?"

Mrs. Dalhousie stops pacing, but her pale brown dress continues to swish around her ankles.

"Don't leave. *Stay.* I'll be right back. You understand? Stay." With that, she hurries out the door, slamming it behind her. There are muffled voices outside; the next set of parents here for interviews, probably. And Mrs. Dalhousie hasn't even said one thing about you yet. Hop backwards onto the desk. Overhead, the ceiling fan whirs and whirs.

"I've been doing fine. You've seen. I passed that test and everything."

Her leaves nod.

"She better not put me in detention. If she puts me in detention, I'll... I'll... well, no. You're right. I shouldn't overreact. You always know best."

The voices outside the door grow louder. Count the ceiling fan's rotations: one, one hundred, two-hundred and one, three hundred...

Finally, Mrs. Dalhousie re-enters, followed by the school principal, Ms. Reinhard. Ms. Reinhard is a cow. She's tall and wide with dyed-red hair cropped short at the sides. Her jacket has shoulder pads.

"Aislinn," Ms. Reinhard says. "I hear there's been some confusion about your mother's interview."

Do a quick scan of the classroom. You could shimmy down the drain pipe outside the window, but the soles of your converse are peeling, which probably messes with their grip. Ms. Reinhard blocks the only doorway. Air vents? No, too narrow.

"I want to go home."

Cradle her in your free arm, her pot somehow heavier than you expected, and swing on your backpack.

"That's just fine," Ms. Reinhart says, but her voice is flat, dead, her voice says, *that's not fine.* "How about I give you a ride? It's a long walk out of town."

"I can walk."

"Please, Aislinn," Mrs. Dalhousie chimes in. Her arms are criss-crossed over her waist, hugging herself. "It's raining."

Look out the window. The sky is suffocated with clouds, an army of them, grey clouds marching on and on into the distance. The rainfall is almost too soft to see.

"Just an in-between rain."

Mrs. Dalhousie and Ms. Reinhart exchange a look.

"Aislinn, we called your neighbour, Mrs. Morrison. She said she hasn't seen your mother in a few weeks. Where is she?"

"Mrs. Morrison is a dumb old hag," you say.

"Aislinn!"

"*Aislinn*, that is unacceptable language. I'm taking you home." Ms. Reinhard storms forwards, arm extended, shoulder pads forming a rigid wall between you and the door. You try and duck around her, but the clay pot in your arm weighs you down, and soon her meaty fingers grip your elbow.

"Let me go! Let me go! I'll kill you! Did you hear me? I'll kill you!"

Howl so loud that you somehow don't notice when Mrs. Dalhousie rushes to her desk and dials 9-1-1. Howl until the police come, and while they try and speak to you in hard, collected voices, these trained killers telling you not to worry, calm down, don't worry, howl until they give up all pretences and cuff your hands behind your back, but howl *loudest*, howl *loudest* when an officer with a nautical star tattooed on his neck picks up mother and carries her out of the room, just like that, she's gone, and it's over, and finally, finally, even though you don't want to, even though you're still writhing and hissing as the police escort you to their car, you begin to cry.

***

They make you leave everything behind except a handful of clean undies and your favorite black dress. We can buy you a new toothbrush, they say. We can buy you a new houseplant.

But I need her.

The officer with the nautical star tattoo shakes his head, places her on your window ledge. Undies. Maybe a stuffed animal, if you've got one. But no plant.

Howl and bite and kick and kick and kick and kick and kick.

Try to make them understand that the person they find in the backyard under the hydrangea isn't her, not anymore. Can't they see she has moved on? Can't they see she's gotten a second chance? Why would they take that away? *Why are you taking her away from me?*

You're grieving, they say.

Press your face against the rear windshield of their blue-and-white car as it bumps out the driveway. Mother sits on the ledge in your bedroom, alone. Already, her leaves sag. Already, she's thirsty. It won't be long now until they come, fat and writing, their tapered bodies forcing their way into her mouth, nose, ears, little red eyes aglow like fiery comets; no, it won't be long, and once they're done with her, once her hands are their hands and her face is their face and her body is their body, once there's nothing left for anyone to remember her by, then, in the night, in a stranger's bed in a stranger's house, then they'll come for you.

THE TREE OF LIFE IN LISBON

OCTAVIA CADE

Octavia Cade is a grad student in science communication. Her short fiction has appeared in Strange Horizons, Cosmos, and Aurealis, and her first novella, the science fiction story "Trading Rosemary," has just been released by Masque Books.

(In Lisbon, the soil is sandy and crumbles beneath her. Eve grows grapes in a walled garden, a Malvasian varietal with green skins that swell in sunlight, and between the rows is lavender. The lavender has bright flowers and leaves that are little spikes that scratch her when she comes to cut the flowers for harvesting. In the corner of the garden nearest her house is a giant cork-oak, and she uses the bark for bottling and for boiling, for stopping wine and for lighting fires beneath cauldrons full of lavender to steam out the oil.)

***

"You are turning into a shut-in," said the Golem. "It is unbecoming."

"It's not a flaw to appreciate the comforts of home," said Eve. "And travelling is so tiresome. It's barely been two centuries since the last move. You cannot be bored yet."

"I could never be bored with you," said the Golem, honey-tongued and reproachful at once. "I lack the capacity."

"I know," said Eve, who had carved lack of imagination into his tongue, who would not see the same mistake made twice. "You should be grateful for that."

"I am not grateful," said the Golem. "And I am not bored. You have not left this garden for decades. I am disturbed."

"I've no reason to leave," said Eve. "I like it here."

"I am disturbed," said the Golem again. Eve heaved a sigh, and with her little carving knife sliced silence into the skin of a sweet, plump little grape and fed it to him, letting herself bask in the quiet. And the Golem did not speak and he did not nag, did not try to convince her to go out to market or to the hairdressers, to the puppet shows or the street musicians. The Golem was used to silence, had been fed it with olives and rose-water and seed pods, the muddy taste of mangroves, and he held the grape carefully on his tongue, carefully between jaws of clay, and waited to be told to spit it out.

He was not capable of boredom, but Eve was.

***

(In Jerusalem, Eve has a garden of pomegranates and anemones, and the flowers and the fruit are red. Red as sunsets, red as blood, and Eve picks the flowers and weaves them into wreaths, into crowns and necklaces because they are beautiful and they make her feel beautiful too. She opens up the pomegranates and rolls the seeds under her tongue, crushes them and paints herself, her lips and cheeks and eyelids, and there are anemones in her hair.)

***

"I'm going out," said Eve. "See? This is me, going out. Are you happy now?"

The Golem stared at her, unblinking.

"Watch the garden for me," she said. Not that it needed much watching now, near full-grown and close to perfect. There was only so much that Eve could do with perfect, and the taste of grapes was beginning to pall. She yearned for a different scent of soap than lavender, but with her face and her figure and her hair all brushed out no one would care what flower she smelled like.

She watched the women first, watched how they moved, how the fabric of new fashion affected their walk, the way that they held themselves. The Golem had procured her a wardrobe, but he could not tell her how much a particular skirt would limit her steps, or how the latest shoes would affect her balance. She could have practiced herself along the garden paths until she could wear with grace what had been provided her, but experience had taught her that accuracy required models and so she mimicked the women around her until she could pass as what they were, until her camouflage was perfect.

She watched the women first, but they were not all that she watched.

***

(Eve builds a stepped garden in Alexandria, stepped down to the river and the garden is built in basins. These are so thick with water lilies, with lotuses, that the crocodiles are clogged by them and cannot push their way through, and Eve can sit near the shallows in peace, without them pressing at her legs and begging for scraps. The flowers are blue in the day, but when evening comes the blue lotuses close up and the white open, night-blooming and scented. And because they are her flowers, Eve can push them apart and bathe herself, rolling in the shallows, and because it is her bathing the crocodiles are considerate and keep onlookers away.)

***

Her excursions are windows; they are never doors. To go too often, to place much consideration on the going, would be to connect her worlds more closely than Eve cares to have them connected. This does not mean that she is unattached herself. Eve has at times spent as much as a day a decade roaming the streets of the cities attached to her gardens. It is as much contact as she cares for, but it is enough.

She goes to see festivals, sometimes, but mostly she goes to watch the ordinary. To see if it has raised itself from disappointment, from the needs and blame of others. To walk streets that are littered and filthy with sewage, to see art and arguments and street brawls, to see poverty and glass houses. Sometimes she has visited places of worship, and they are nearly all made of stone and silence and the absence of growing things, and she thinks that disobedience has led to a different world than she had ever dreamed.

"You are the one who is always looking back," said the Golem, but he was mistaken. Her gardens are not recreations, or not only so.

"I am looking forward," she said to him. "One creation at a time. There is a time to plant, Golem, and there is a time to reap. I have been planting for a long time."

"Is there an end to the planting?" said the Golem.

"Yes," said Eve, thinking of the world that had been built, the world where she walked behind, and thinking too of the world she wished to plant about her. "But not soon."

***

(In Athens, Eve grows fruit trees—lemons and olives and almonds, and all of these she preserves in great jars, but for the first the preservation is secondary. She grows the lemons for their colour but their taste is not to hers and so she leaves the jars on the street, outside her door and at dawn. One night, the jar is broken before it is taken, and Eve stops preserving and lets the fruit fall, breaks their roundness open with her heels until the whole garden is lemon-scented and juicy with it.)

***

The Golem had been an early creation. Made from mud herself, from the ribs of mud, Eve knew the touch of clay, how it could be bound together and bound to. She had not built the Golem from her gardens, from the earth buried there and homely. Rather she had bought the clay a piece at a time, kept it soft and wet until the shape of its conglomerate spoke to her and she was able to build something to breathe life into: a heavy shape with skin as dark as her own and loyal as she had not been to anyone other than herself.

"Do you love me?" she said to the Golem, one evening early in the onset of its life. It was not an idle curiosity: Eve had carved lack where bones might have been, but this Golem was not the first.

"I do not love you," said the Golem.

"Do you think I want you to?" she said.

The Golem looked at her, considering. "No," he said, and Eve was satisfied.

"I am not a kind person, Golem," she said. "I will not always be kind to you. But that is one cruelty I will not stoop to."

***

(Her garden in Byzantium is walled, and in it Eve grows roses and poppies and mint. The roses for their water, the poppies for their dreams and the mint for her drinks, and she lies in the sun, baking to the sounds of the city around her, the clash and clatter of markets, and within the walls her flesh is scented and cool and dozes, while the Golem strips away thorns and bleeds seed pods and mixes the mint with wine and honey. All the plants are in pots, and between them the paths are made of mortar and mosaics, of shards of shattered marble.)

***

In Lisbon, Eve visited wharfs where great ships embarked on

exploration, and the prospect of a new world, of new gardens, was not a foreign one, nor unattractive. She visited palaces and fish markets and Belém Tower, the Carmo Convent, saw the quiet chapels, the library, but although the rose window was beautiful it did not compare with the roses she had grown.

She visited the Opera House, the Phoenix Opera, nine months before it was burnt down, razed by fire and earthquake, and when she visited it was not yet open and still unfinished. One of the workmen recognised her—she had come to him before, once in his youth and once again when there was more grey in his hair than black. He showed her the stage, the dressing rooms, the foundations, and more besides.

"Him again?" said the Golem, when Eve came back with her dress not nearly as perfect as when she had left. "That has not worked so well with you before."

"Maybe this time will be different," said Eve, caressing her belly. "Either way, it is the last time. They grow old so quickly, poor things."

"You are becoming a sentimentalist," said the Golem.

"If you had a heart you would also have favourites," said Eve, who remembered her favourites best, the way they strained and built and bloomed around her.

***

(Eve's garden in Great Zimbabwe is a place of shifting and shadows, of grass and rock and sculpture, shaded with trees that smell of turpentine, that scatter seed-pods and have leaves like butterfly wings. She stacks stone in the shape of Golems and leaves them unmortared, rings them with thin circles of grass shaped into the earth like letters, strings them with glass beads and porcelain and gold coins. When the Golem stands among them their surfaces are different but the shadows they cast are the same, and the grass brushes up against them both and whispers.)

***

The first time that Eve sees him, she desires him.

She wonders if he has ever had a woman before. He is so very young. His skin is even smoother than hers, and it amuses her that though she is thousands of years his senior, anyone looking at them would count the difference on less than one hand.

The first time he touches her she is surprised, for his hands are rougher than the rest of him, and his palms have the flavour of stone. He is an apprentice, he tells her. One bound to masonry, and when she runs her fingers through his hair she can feel the traces of ground marble. "You have to be careful with it," he says. "You have to know where to cut. Mistakes are expensive."

"Don't I know it," says Eve. She feeds him wine, little sips of it while he's still underneath her, still inside her, and if the wine is raw in his mouth, innocent of cellars and too young on the vines then he is too inexperienced to know it. His intoxication is from other sources. "This is my first harvest," she says of the liquor, too pale in the glass, taken from thin vines. There had been no more than a handful of grapes. "It came from my own garden."

There is dirt underneath her fingernails, still.

***

Eve thinks the second time a whim. It is something she has done before—not often, but it does happen. It amuses her to think that she has fucked the same flesh, with a different inhabitant. The mason only believes he is the same person. There is some similarity in the features, though his skin has lost its smoothness, though his hair is greyed and his form thicker—but he is grown now, and the decades between him and the boy he was make him different than he was before. Or so Eve feels, when she makes love to him and the body beneath her feels new, exciting. As if she were meeting him again, for the first time.

"It's true, I am not the same," he says. "I have been a father these past two decades."

"Oh?" says Eve, who had the Golem drop off the boy at the paternal doorstep. "Well. These things happen." She rocks above him, feels his hands grip her hips and still her. His fingers press so hard there will be bruises in her flesh.

"These things happen?" he says.

"A child needs a home," she says. "Is that not the way of it?" If this night's child were also a boy, she would wrap him carefully in soft fabric, swaddle him in silk, send him out into a place for orphans, or a family looking to foster. Perhaps to the mason, again, if the babe had the hands for it. "And a boy needs a father."

"If it were a girl?"

"I have never had a daughter I did not have to bury," she says, and that makes his eyes soften as she hoped it would, loosens his grip on her body. It makes other things soften as well, so Eve leans over him, lets her hair fall around his face in a haze of lavender and fastens her mouth, all redolent with wine, against his own. She moves against him again, slow and urgent.

Softness does not suit her.

***

"You haven't changed a day," he says, spreading his hands wide in supplication, in confession. "You see the same is not true for me." His face is old, his skin wrinkled and heavy and the truth of his words is written all over him.

There are many things that she could say. "I would know you anywhere," or "You are not so different." "Your hands are as they have always been," perhaps. Eve says none of them. They would *all be lies. The Golem has told her of the Opera, of the way it climbs upwards, of the way it lies heavy on the earth. This is not something that interests her, a pretence of a growing thing that holds no green, that does not ripen. What she does remember is a man who worked with stone as if it were plants, as if it were gardens and grafting and knowledge.*

When that man lies underneath her again it is as if it were the first time, all over again. As if he were another man. There have been so many. He would not be out of place. She saves the wine, this time, sweet and heavy and perfect, saves it because he is old now and it takes more than her blooming to rouse him. He is a flower himself, quick to wilt at the first sign of bruising, of unkind treatment and alcohol. It is something for them to share when the lovemaking is over and his seed sticky-safe inside her. "I remember this taste," he says. "I think it is better now, though perhaps that is just an old man's fancy."

"No," says Eve. "It comes from a garden that is just as it should be."

When she leaves, for the last time, he presses into her palm a small stone flower, carved from marble with green veins all through it. "It's beautiful," says Eve.

"I did not know if you would come back," he says, and the knowledge is between them that she will not do so again. "Keep it to remember me by."

"I will keep it," says Eve.

(She doesn't.)

***

(In Prague, Eve plants flowers—a carpet of bellflowers and windflowers and helleborine. She picks the flowers one by one, plucks at each petal in a game of love-me-not and sighs. So much destruction leaves her hands sticky, and she buries the denuded heads under a linden tree, under the heavy scent and the beehives and lies with her skirt full of blue and white petals and her palms open to the sky, letting the bees crawl over her and dust her skin with pollen.)

***

The first Golem she made could not speak, so Eve shattered it so that something, at least, would break the silence, and used pieces of the body as pavestones. It was years before wear rounded the cobbles to comfortable shapes. She still had the scars on her heels.

The second Golem could not walk. The third was too afraid to dig lest its big clay hands be ruined. The fourth was nervous around fire. The fifth was too careless of apples, the sixth wanted nothing more than to drool and eat dirt.

The second she used as a trellis, the third she turned into a birdbath. The fourth she softened with water until it returned to mud, the fifth she dismantled and rebuilt as a cider press. The sixth she let eat, until its greedy child-Golem self was stuffed too full of dirt and exploded into fine grains of fertiliser.

It was a learning process, but Eve didn't want something created to be dependent, something she would always have to look after. She did not want to be needed; she did not want the obligation.

She valued her own competence too much to hamstring competence in others.

The seventh Golem spoke too much and was clever with sponge baths. Eve gave him a key to the garden gate—the keys to a succession of garden gates—and he tucked the key inside his cheek and wandered out into the city, into a city, one after another. He always came back.

Eve was not sure which of them was the more surprised.

***

(In Songo Mnara, her garden is confined to a courtyard, and a semi-open one at that. Eve stands the Golem in the door-way and his big body hides her plants, hides the stones she has dug up to make room for root systems. The garden walls are coral blocks and shining lime, and there are statuaries there, and the scent of mangroves. There are pearls and silks and a little trickling pool, and the trees that Eve plants for shade are cool-fruited coconut palms and the thick bulging trunks of baobabs.)

***

The final birth in Lisbon coincided with earthquakes and water and fire. She'd have liked to take it as a joke, but that would have required a sense of humour so dark it was beyond her, although she thought that the Golem might have appreciated it.

But earthquakes were ephemeral, so Eve dug her fingers into the earth and brought forth in pain. "Push," said the Golem, and she was used to pushing and to pushing out, her hands clawing at the earth as they had first clawed in the first garden, when she was pushed out with leaves clutched in her hands and twigs under her fingernails, remnants from the tree of life and death, the tree she had not eaten from. Later, she would graft these undying fragments to the tree she had tasted, raised from the seeds she had eaten in the garden. Seeds that had passed through her body and come out soft-ened and ready for planting.

"Push," said the Golem, and "Oh, for fuck's sake," Eve replied, panting and filthy and remembering all over again just how much she hated labour. Then the child was crown-ing and out and "It's a girl," said the Golem, "and about time too."

"You're telling me," said Eve, listening to the grinding earth and the fire and the shrieks. "Would you listen to that racket?

If we had to stay here any longer there wouldn't be a moment's peace."

***

(In Maidstone, Eve plants apples and nothing else. Her orchards spread before her, heavy with blossom and fragrant. The apples are red and yellow and green, the fruit shining in the sun like jewels, and she plants them in spirals, in great flowering mazes and she wanders through them crunching apples with her hard bright teeth and sucking the juice from her fingers. She lets the seeds drop behind her like breadcrumbs, and at the centre of the orchards is another tree, another apple, and this is red and green and yellow at once, a perfect grafting, and she gobbles these apples like marchpane, like subtleties, and saves the seeds for planting.)

***

When Eve smothered her daughter in Lisbon, she was on her hands and knees and with the earth still trembling beneath. It was a feast day, and the normal sounds of celebration had been replaced by screams and the heavy rush of water, but Eve knew that the garden was safe, that the water couldn't touch her and the ground beneath would stay unsplit, so she did not choose to hurry. It was more important to pat the earth into place than to hurry. More important to cover up that little face gently, so gently, so that it would not be damaged, and to place the seed of grafted apples on the small and silent chest, a stone flower in the tiny cold hand. "Don't worry, little one," she said to her daughter. "The fire can't hurt you, nor can anything else. The tree will keep the garden safe until you're ready to do it yourself."

When the seed grew into a tree, there would be the fruit of life and death, the fruit of knowledge, and when that fruit dropped into the root-exposed mouth of the child it would

wake and break open the rich, apple-infused earth above
it and the garden would have a guardian again. Someone
strong, someone to weed and plant and wait until the world
that Eve was building was ready for her. A woman's world,
this time, where all the trees were in bounds and the only sin
lay in the stifling and limitation of others.

"Really?" said the Golem, when she informed him of such.
"What was it that happened to my brothers, again?"

***

(In Marrakesh, Eve plants cedar and cypress and apricots.
She likes the way that their trunks rise about her, the way
that the trees make her feel safe and shaded. The Golem
helps her to build a little pavilion and Eve carves palm trees
into the stone and gorges herself on apricots. She waits until
they're plump and sugar-sticky with bright juice, devours the
flesh and buries the clean stones in clusters around the qanat
wells and channels.)

***

Weakened as she was from the birth, Eve was done with the
burial, with her goodbyes, before the screams and the swells
and the shakings were over. "This is most inconvenient," she
said to the Golem as he stripped her of the filthy birthing
clothes, as he cleansed her of blood and earth and sweat and
scented her with lavender water, gave her wine to drink from
a bottle that had not yet broken.

"It will be difficult to hire porters," said the Golem, lacing
strong shoes onto her feet so that she could not be cut by
fragments of crockery and glass, the hard ragged edges of
fallen masonry. "And there is only so much I can carry."

"Then we'll just take what's most important," said Eve. "The
seeds, of course, and gold. Once we're out of the city it will

be easier to find transportation. I don't know about you, Golem, but I feel the sudden need to be somewhere else."

"Where are we going?" said the Golem. "Madrid, Bilbao, Bordeaux?"

"I think not," said Eve. "I think this time I would like to go south. We have not been south for such a long time."

"There is a lot of south," said the Golem. He would have said it had been a hard birth, that she needed to rest, but Eve had her little carving knife still and if there were no grapes left in the garden there was glass on the floors, glass that could be scratched and swallowed and this was not a time for silence.

"We have plenty of time," said Eve. "And you have always said I should travel more."

When she locked the garden gate behind her for the final time, and went out into the ruins of Lisbon, the garden shimmered behind her and was gone.

"You'd never know it was there," said the Golem.

"Of course not," said Eve, who had known knowledge and its lack, who had known life and its ending and who had little tolerance for bald displays of power. "That's the point."

***

(In Wellington, Eve's garden is pohutukawa and cabbage trees, bright red flowers with fronds like strands of blood and spiking leaves that stand bold against the sky. There are kowhai that bloom in brief waves of gold, kowhai that entice the tui to her garden, their feathers green-black and shot through with purple. There are toetoe and flaxes and ferns, and her garden is hidden by hills. The pohutukawa are her favourite: they cling to crevices on the hillside, make their homes on cliffs and precarious places, and though they shift in the wind they do not fall.

Eve carves their blossoms out of clay and swallows them whole; carves words upon their leaves and feeds them to the Golem and is happy.)

EXALTED GUESTS
(OR HOW MALKA RAISED A DYBBUK ARMY)

RENA ROSSNER

Rena Rossner lives in Jerusalem where she
works as a literary agent. She is a writer of
both fiction and poetry. Her cookbook,
Eating the Bible (Skyhorse Publishing) is
now out in five languages.

It happened quite by accident, the first time Malka raised a dybbuk army. It was the holiday of Sukkot, of the Tabernacle year and she had wandered down into Safed's ancient cemetery. All the night's ghosts had already been conjured. The ushpizin were carousing from home-made bamboo shelter to sheeted tent and palm-frond hut. Malka figured the cemetery would be empty, a place away from all the noise and song. She had had enough of all the holidays, too much food and togetherness, too much raptured prayer and forgiveness of sin.

As she wandered down the lonely city's narrow lanes, she got further and further away from her family's Sukkah. She drifted away from her father and mother, her siblings whose holiday finery was by now hopelessly stained with meatball sauce and dust. Her hand rested on each tombstone as she walked, her skirt hem brushed each granite-covered grave. The wind had obviously responded to the afternoon's rain-prayer and she could smell the moisture in the air.

Malka closed her eyes and let the fingers of the wind stroke her face. The rain began and tickled Malka's arms. She laughed, softly at first and then louder, risking her forbidden voice in the breeze. And then she felt the presence. It was chilling in a different way than rain and wind—a presence in her spine. It was a faint pressure, like a palm pressed gently at the small of her back, but from the inside. Forbidden. She tasted lightning on her tongue—smoky, slightly burnt. It had the heady scent of a havdalah candle—only just extinguished in Saturday-night wine, full of promise and cloves.

The next thing she knew she was howling, like something fierce had been released from within her. And even though she knew that she wasn't exactly the one making those sounds, she felt wild and free. She danced and spun among the monuments, the turquoise skull-capped mausoleums that were the shrines of long-dead rabbis, the tzaddikkim. She sang the songs of men. The songs her father chanted in the synagogue, the kabbalistic incantations she was supposed to only hear, not speak. And it all rolled off her tongue in wild cantillation, sounding everything and nothing like a hymn.

Her hair lashed out, wet now, untamed. Her eyes: red-rimmed, angry. And she knew the wrath of the forgotten. She felt them all around her. The ones who never got invited. They simmered underground, trembling in silent rage. And with the voice of a forbidden one inside her, Malka knew them all: their names, their dates of death, their pain. They all spoke at once, threatening rift and disillusion. They creeped their earthworm-slow way, in the direction of Safed's fault line.

And Malka, who was not-Malka, but aware of both her newfound body and its host, now knew that earthquakes here could happen in an instant, and they had nothing to do with rifts beneath the ground. And so she raised them all. She called to them by name. "Reb Dov ben Eliezer, Hannale bat Esther, Shlomo ben Harav Meir, Shayna bat Leah, Perel Beila bat Rivka, Avraham ben Natan," and more. She crooned and wailed in voices not her own, in languages she'd heard but never spoken, spitting letters like curses onto the ground.

They rose. Sisters, brothers, fathers, mothers, tiny babies, and great-but-since-forgotten Rabbis, thieves and drunkards, whores and scholars, the righteous, the sinful, the soldiers, the cripples, she raised a dybbuk army. And then she turned her back on them and walked back up the mountain, singing. The swirling horde followed her lead. They sang a niggun, a dirge, dancing on the shears of wind. And when she reached the holy city, first she took them to her home. Her family had long since finished eating. The men sang songs and drank hot sweet mint tea and with the wind and rain she ripped the sukkah open, and in her new-found shrieking voice she called: "I invite to my meal the exalted guests" and named them all.

She saw the looks on all their faces, her father Yosef, her brothers: Rafael, Shimon and Daniel. She saw her mother's eyes dawn in recognition, the names she called at once familiar and strange. Her grandmother fainted. Her little sisters woke up from the benches where they had gone to sleep.

"May it please you, my exalted guests, that all the other exalted guests dwell with me and with you," she finished, and with her voice she swept them in. They danced around the table, fanning the candle flames. They licked the icing on the sheet-cake and dipped their noses in the tea. Malka saw what no one else did, until the candles flickered and the rain took a deep breath. It was an instant, an eye-blink, the space between two heartbeats and the dybbuks flew in through every nostril.

That's when the howling began in earnest. The frenzied song of the unhinged. The forgotten spoke so loudly that the town began to come. Slowly first, they peeked out of their home-made booths, but with the rise in shattered melody, they coursed on down through stair-lined streets. Malka laughed each time a chin fell, she giggled into every open-mouth, she snapped her fingers and they followed, a dybbuk for each resident, a forgotten one made whole.

It was the women she called loudest. Malka left the men to whirl. Naked with their payot flying, fur-lined streimels cast into the air. She took the women by their hands and led them to the shul. There she opened up the aron, the holy torah-ark. And as the women plundered all the prayer-desks, longing to see what really lay inside those holes, Malka took out all the shawls. She draped each woman with a tallit, and with these shrouds they howled more. Ghost-like in their frenzy, banshees finally released, the women calmed as Malka hushed them, and with reverence removed the scrolls. Ten torahs she took out and passed them, until each woman had a turn to feel its weight. Not of babies or of soup-pots, but of holy written words. And then the niggun really started, led by one of the little girls. Brachaleh bat Esther sang a dirge in grand-hasidic style. And the women-dybbuks danced around the bimah, no longer forgotten or afraid.

The men outside came in to see it, dripping wet and naked to the hilt. They climbed the stairs up to the women's section, and watched wide-eyed from every balconette. They kept silent, for the first time. They watched their wives and daughters dance and sing, and even though their dybbuk souls were restless, they sat long enough to take it in.

Soon the women finished their carousing, the torahs kissed unabashedly and then returned. The men swarmed out of shul to heed the calling of the wind. The women shrieked their way out of the windows, they met the men out on the rooftops for the night, and every sukkah-house was visited, each and every cookie licked. But then they meted out destruction. Razing palm-frond roofs, collapsing sheds. The dybbuk army wouldn't stop, until every sukkah started falling, and everyone remembered them.

Malka sat atop the synagogue. Her long blue dress was torn to shreds. She felt the warming sun begin ascent. She twirled her drying hair between her fingers, and spat the rain back through her teeth. She sang a lonely melody, a requiem that to the cats sounded like one in pain. And then she wandered down the alleys, back down the winding stairs and through the earthquake-ravaged city's many falling stones.

She wandered through the gravestones as before, and climbed onto the tallest dome. She shrieked this time with both her voices, both dybbuk-speak and human tone. She called her army home. And one by one they came to her, out of body orifices the swarm escaped. Each soul-like shadow made its own dramatic exit, out of nostril, ear, eye, anus, hole and pore, each human staring at Malka in wonder, then wondering where went their clothes.

Malkah tucked in every dybbuk, smoothing down the granite stones and then she birthed the one inside her, tearing through her virgin core. She kissed her, lip on lip, and shed a tear. Then Malka wandered homeward, following the human tide. Each one to their deserted bed returned, where they slept and dreamt the dreams of the forgotten, and woke remembering nothing but a storm.

PEACHES IN THE BREEZE

SIOBHAN GALLAGHER

Siobhan Gallagher is a wannabe zombie slayer, currently residing in the Forever City. Her fiction has appeared in several publications, including AE - The Canadian Science Fiction Review, On Spec, Abyss & Apex, Unidentified Funny Objects anthology, and Grimdark Magazine.

"Peaches in the Breeze" was originally published in Abyss & Apex.

If she kills the man with the red-jeweled hand, they might all go free. The snakes in her hair whisper hope, never promises. Yet...

Freedom.

She mouths the word, imagines the taste of a ripe peach chilled by the stream, the peach softness of her sister's cheek. Her reflexes, quick as a serpent, have never failed her.

She slips the blade inside her kimono and paints her face, kohl around her eyes, ruby lips to match the warlord's gem. He will want her lips on his hand. Her snakes weave among her hair, lie against her scalp, still as scaled combs.

At sunset, she joins the other girls outside the warlord's home, waiting to be chosen. None desire to be here. Tears flow down their faces, smearing the paint. One will die, so that their village may live another day.

This has to stop.

The warlord and his entourage approach on horseback, returning from a day of pillaging. His men are drunk, but he is wary even in victory. Others have tried to kill a daimyo. She bares her shoulders, and hides her face behind a fan of crimson and gold, a subtle play for his attention. His dark eyes are on her. He points, and his men take her.

***

Surrounded by four paper walls, she sits, hands in her lap. The warlord enters, filling the space with his bulk. She rises and bows. He circles her, leering, fingers on his sheathed katana. Does he know? She bows lower, hiding fear. The snakes squirm and her hair ripples.

He halts, scowling, and motions for her to remove her clothing. He sees her knife as her robes hit the floor. His katana whines through the air, but she is faster. Her steel fang pierces his side.

There's no blood.

She jerks away. The warlord laughs and lunges at her, katana whistling. She stumbles back, crashes through the paper wall and into the moonlight.

She blinks. Her headless body lies inches from her face.

The snakes writhe, their venom sinking into her scalp. It courses through her, burning, gnawing. It's energy, it's fire. She glares at the warlord with the intensity of poison.

He's paralyzed; can't breathe. And he falls like a wall of stone.

She smiles, and closes her eyes for the last time.

From her neck emerges a serpent, pearl-white scales and ruby eyes shimmering under the moon. It tongues the air, tastes peaches in the breeze, and glides toward home.

SOWING RUBIES FOR BRIDES

(OR THE GRAVEYARD ON THE EDGE OF FAERYLAND)

SUZANNE J. WILLIS

Suzanne is a Melbourne based writer and a graduate of
Clarion South. Her short stories have appeared or are
forthcoming in Goldfish Grimm's Spicy Fiction Sushi,
Schlock Magazine, Postscripts by PS Publishing, and
anthologies by Prime Books, Fablecroft Publishing and
Kayelle Press. She works full-time and writes in the
spaces around it, inspired by fairytales, ghost stories
and all things strange. Suzanne can be found online at
suzannejwillis.webs.com

Tirra stands at the edge of the field that she had sown three weeks earlier, watching ribbons push up from the earth and fly in the wind over the graveyard, the Murky Woods and, beyond that, across the ephemeral border between this world and Faeryland. Spell-ribbon for old-school witches. Soft pink ribbon for ballet shoes that will dance all night. Blue ribbon for tying boxes filled with stars. The air is filled with them, spiralling and dipping in the early morning light. This will be fine crop, she thinks, slinging the seed bag across her body and striding out across the day, the uncut rubies tinkling like tiny bells inside the coarse fabric. Are the seeds rubies, or the rubies seeds? After all these years, harvest after harvest, it doesn't seem to matter. Between Tirra, the poppies that grow from the faery graves and the bees that pollinate the poppies' ruby seeds, faery brides continue to grow here on the edge of Faeryland. There are no jewel-bright flashes of the bees among the ribbons this morning, but perhaps they're among the poppies, instead.

Begin planting the next crop as soon as the ribbons fly from the first, her mother, Raewyn, told her long ago. So in the next field over, Tirra walks across the loamy soil, the sky wheat-gold above her and the honey-heavy smell of summer breezing past.

The rubies scatter across the earth, anywhere but the carefully lined furrows, and wriggle themselves into the soil. It doesn't bother Tirra, for the seeds must do as they want to do. She smiles as her shadow skips along, singing to the ruby seeds in its oboe-low voice and listening for the happy burbling beneath the soil as they take root as creatures fresh and new. Her shadow is Tirra-shaped, of course, but wraith-shoots like climbing sweetpeas curl from its shoulders, hips, fingertips. It is happy to be out in the sunlight after its hibernation. Even shadows need their rest in this land.

The last of the ribbons twirl through the air and are lost from sight. Thick green stalks are waving in their place and the shadows that grow on them—dwarves and winged monkeys, worry-dolls to whisper children to sleep, women with the tails of snakes and hearts of daemons—will soon shake themselves free and follow the ribbons, to do bidding as wishes and dreams. Then, as the stalks wither and begin to compost, the crop of faery brides will pull themselves from the earth and knock at Tirra's door, eager to claim their prizes. Why do they see human men as prizes, especially after the terrible Bride Hunts of yesteryear? Still, there has never been one who hasn't gone willingly to her marriage. The fae are made of stronger stuff than any ordinary folk.

Tirra remembers the horror of 1872—she was only a girl then—and the rows of dead fae that were the first she and her mother buried. She remembers the murderers who organised hunting faery brides for sport and Raewyn's decree that their punishment was to wander forever in the Tangled Maze. She remembers everything.

Tirra reaches the iron fence that surrounds the graveyard at the end of the field. It stretches out before her, irregular rows of tombstones and free-standing glass panes bordered in iron and filled with pressed-flowers, vellum love notes, locks of hair from long-dead fae. Although it is summer, the trees scattered between the graves are bare of their leaves. Snow lays in the shadows of the gravestones, stark against the blood-red poppies swaying gently in the afternoon. The seasons do not behave normally within the graveyard. Then again, neither do the dead.

Something isn't right—it is too quiet, with none of the familiar buzzing of bees filling the air. Tirra's shadow trembles as she opened the gate. "You can stay here, if you like," she says. The shadow nods and sits down to wait, and Tirra walks through the gate alone. The earth feels different here. The fae rest in graves surrounded by iron fences to keep out old enemies who might want to feast on the corpses and end the marriages between fae and humans forever.

She whispers to the dead as she walks, reminiscing about the tin children who rusted under the earth and emerged again as a flock of silvery moths when it came time to harvest the poppies surrounding their graves. That whole crop of brides was petulant, with shining white hair. So different to the swan-women, who were buried in pairs—the poppies that grew over those graves had onyx seeds, instead of dark rubies, producing brides who went to men in need of a firm wife to keep them in line. Most, though, give rise to the poppies across the graveyard that perfume the air bitter and sweet, and whose ruby-seeds Tirra harvests then sows into the earth.

Even though the sun is warm and the poppies sway, Tirra shivers. From the Murky Woods float the sounds of jazz and the rattle of glasses. Nothing wrong there. In the field behind her, shoots push up through the earth from the wriggling seeds, just as they should. But her fears are confirmed—the bees have disappeared. Not one of the shiny amethyst and emerald insects bumbles through the air from the woods, to the poppies, back to the hive under the old sycamore tree. Heart pounding, Tirra runs towards the tree.

***

A breeze blows the sycamore leaves around Tirra as she sinks to the ground beneath the tree. Her throat tightens and tears

well in her eyes as she presses her hands gently onto the
bones that were long-ago bleached white by the elements.
The gryphon's skeleton has lain here ever since she was small
girl. She had been charged with sitting with the gryphon
until the creature's death, stroking her fur and listening
to her breathing getting shallower. Tirra had sat with her
throughout the night, as the moon passed across the sky and
the sun rose again, when the last breath rattled through the
old one's body.

The bones are sun-warmed. Here are forepaw bones, still
tipped with claws too sharp to touch. There, the skull
rests, grass and summer daisies garlanding the teeth and
eyesockets. Most importantly, lying gently against the
roots of the sycamore is the huge ribcage—but it is too still
without the pale blue beehive that the ribs should safely
encase. Instead, it is empty, with no sign of its bees which
pollinate the graveyard's poppies. There is nothing but
silence, a cool wind and Tirra's fear.

This place was made sacred by the gryphon's death, for faery
bees need faery bones in which to build their hives. No bees
means no more poppies with their ruby seeds. No more ruby
seeds means no more faery brides. And no more brides means
the worlds will sicken again. Tirra wipes away her tears and
stands up. There is no-one else here but her and the fae at
their rest—fat lot of good they're going to do me, she thinks.
She looks across the graveyard and back toward the field,
then over to the woods. But there is no clue as to who might
have stolen the hive.

The sycamore rustles, a little irritably, and more leaves swirl
around her. Perhaps she should consult the books back at
the house? She feels a soft tapping on her ankle. Her shadow
has slunk in, after all, and is pointing towards the sycamore's
roots. A tiny movement and Tirra sees a lone bee, a tiny amethyst jewel left behind looking for a trail to follow. It leaves

a tiny purple trail of pollen in Tirra's palm as she picks it up. Holding it to her mouth, she whispers to it then watches as it takes flight. Tirra and her shadow run after it, towards the Murky Woods.

***

In the dim green light of the woods the bee's indigo light pulses just ahead, its flight erratically purposeful. Soft verdant moss covers the tree trunks and limns the stone pathways. Tirra is careful not to step on the dead bees that litter the path in a macabre bread-crumb trail. Hidden among the foliage are statues of faery brides of times past, wrapped in vines and the sparkling dew that never quite evaporates. Skeins of hair, silver-blonde, raven-black, flame-red, hang from tree boughs, tributes and offerings to the brides who have gone before. The light shifts and the skeins become fish scales, feathers, fox tails. Tirra feels as though the statues are watching her, disapproving of her failure to keep the hive safe.

She follows the bee as it alights on crumbling stone fountains, moon blossoms and tendrils of mist from across the border that have become something more corporeal in the ordinary world. A familiar buzzing just ahead grows louder as she leaves the path and follows the bee past a copse of yew trees and into a little clearing beyond, behind which a stream gurgles past.

The bee flits across to the far side of the clearing, to join its mates in the blue beehive propped against a tree. Her gut clenches; the hive has been split almost in two. The bees crawl frantically in and out of the hole, and golden honey spills out onto the grass and over the small axe lying next to it on the ground. Just to its left sits a mortal man with an old canvas bag by his side, head bowed and buried in his hands, which are nastily swollen with countless beestings.

"What do you think you're playing at?" Tirra asks through clenched teeth, although doesn't move any closer as the axe is within the man's reach. He looks up and she sees his eyes are red, as though he has been weeping.

"She left me," he says quietly.

Bride trouble, Tirra thinks and knows that caution is imperative. She peers at him. He does seem familiar. There is something about his voice, too, soft and plaintive—

"Your name is Pieter, no? 'A bride with hair of flame, strong limbs, cunning mind and winning smile'." She recites his wish from memory, as she remembers the wishes of all the men to whom her brides have been betrothed.

"Her name was Ilwyn. She was everything to me. I tried to make her happy...then last week, she discovered this." He picks up the canvas bag next to him and tips it up. Red pelts scatter onto the ground, the fur still thick and glossy, tails like bottle brushes and legs tipped in sharp black claws.

Hot anger rises in Tirra: her shadow is shaking. "You mean to tell me that you asked for a cunning faery wife with red hair and you keep the *fox pelts of dead faery brides* in your home?" Her voice is low with fury.

"They belonged to my great-grandfather. I didn't even know I still had them. I'm not proud of my family's involvement in the Bride Hunts, but it was so long ago..."

Tirra's thoughts race, blocking out Pieter's ramblings. First the gangs brought brides over from Faeryland and hunted them for sport. Then, their false cries—"Nicolita spoiled our cow's milk" and "Siobahn took my babe and left a changeling behind"—gave them an excuse to kill even more. She and her mother buried so many of them in the graveyard, fae bled out through bullet wounds in their chests or necks that had been inflicted on them in their animal forms. The swan maiden's white skin splattered in red, the wolf women's beautiful caramel-coloured limbs destroyed by hunters' arrows and knives. The agreement for faery brides to be reborn from dead fae had been the only chance at mending the wounds between this world and Faeryland. Somewhere deep inside, Tirra's anger explodes and next she knows, she is holding Pieter by his throat, against a large stone boulder as his feet dangle uselessly a foot off the ground.

"And now you've come to finish the job?" She feels an anxious little pat on her leg—her shadow points to Pieter, who is red and spluttering, unable to draw breath. Dropping him, she leans down to cup her hand in the flowing stream and holds the water to his mouth. Furious she may be, but she won't turn herself into a murderer because of him.

He coughs, draws in deep breaths, shakes his head at Tirra. "I was just so lonely."

At her feet, Tirra's shadow comforts Pieter's. She sits down between him and the hive.

"Well, faery brides are no cure for loneliness, there's nothing surer," she says.

"The night she found them," he points towards the lifeless pelts strewn across the ground, "I've never seen anyone so angry. She took one of them and stormed out the front door. She stood on the porch and flung it across her shoulders...and then she wasn't there anymore. Instead there was a fox that ran so quickly away from me, into the trees beyond, and in the moonlight, it was just the shade of her hair." He shakes his head again, rubs at the stings on his hands.

"You know that they all leave sooner or later, don't you Pieter? This is their chance for another life! Some disappear in the dead of night, slipping out as quiet as shy ghosts, others in a flurry of anger, casting curses at all and sundry. If they find their skins, they'll be gone faster than you can call their name, off to live in the wilds of our world in their animal form." And the rare ones, she remembers silently, are called back to Faeryland and disappear in a swarm of jewelled bees, the light refracting through their wings and staining the ground, leaving behind their only daughter to mourn the loss and tend the graveyard that is the one link between the two worlds. She sighs and leans over to the stream again.

"Here," she says, tipping water over his hands, the swelling immediately dissipating. "So, trying to destroy my beehive was all for nought—you may want to have your revenge against me for your lost Ilwyn, but she would have gone, anyway."

He laughs gently. "I don't want revenge. I love her and don't want to see her or her sisters risk themselves. I want to make good for what the old bride hunters did, once and for all. No more faery wives to be hunted down. No more of them for this world." Pieter jumps up and heads towards the beehive, looking fierce enough to finish what he has started.

Tirra whispers quickly to her shadow, which snakes away from her. All the shadows in the clearing—the dappling from the canopy, the long shapes of the tree-trunks, the squat darkness beneath the boulders, even Pieter's lithe shape—move across to the abandoned pelts. The skins puff up as though breath has been pumped into them; the darkness fills them up and they stretch their spindle-thin legs, run toward the hive and overtake Pieter. Ears pricked up and dark light staring out from the empty eye sockets, six shadowy little foxes are now blocking his way, snarling and snapping at his ankles.

He stops. "We can't let you do that, Pieter. Our worlds are symbiotic—destroy that hive and you will destroy everything as your great-grandfather and his friends nearly did," Tirra says. When the fae stopped coming and banned mortals from Faeryland, the crops really did fail and women became barren. All the colour bled from both worlds. The two each need a little of the other in order to survive and the graveyard became the link between them.

All her anger towards Pieter is gone. She understands loneliness and abandonment. She knows what it is to love the fae, only to have them slip away and wonders if it is worse to lose a wife or a mother. "What if I grant you a chance to get Ilwyn back?"

He turns and smiles hopefully. The foxes stop yapping but still stand guard around the hive, wary. Bees land on their ears and tails, only to be flicked gently away.

"What would you say to a quest, Pieter?"

***

Tirra sits under the sycamore as the sky turns gold and pink under the setting sun. The bees have calmed and are lazily buzzing around the gryphon's bones as she carefully mends the hive with a finger-bone needle and strands of Pieter's hair. Sacrifice, after all, is part of any good quest, as is burden and boon, by way of the pelts she has directed him to take along. It is up to him whether they will secure his safe passage or his doom.

She and her shadow sing softly, the gentle magic of their song helping to knit the hive back together and bind it to the bones. Somewhere deep in the woods, their song echoes and sighs.

Her shadow cocks its head questioningly at her.

"No," Tirra says, "I don't think he'll like what he finds there. But he has to try. That's how the stories go, isn't it?" She walks back toward the path, her shadow whispering to the bees as they go. Perhaps they will carry the stories to her mother, but she can never be sure.

She wonders if Pieter will find jewelled boxes with the pearl tears of princesses inside? Will he be imprisoned by giants with golden geese and singing harps? Will Ilwyn forgive him or will he search forever for his lost fox-wife? Most of all, she wonders if he will meet a fae queen who is part sylph, part bee, who was once the faery bride and mother who charged her half-mortal daughter with bringing magic back to the ordinary world and the ordinary back to Faeryland.

BROTHER, UNSEEN
SYLVIA HEIKE

Sylvia Heike lives in Finland with her fiancé and pet rabbits. Her writing has appeared in Flash Fiction Magazine, Mad Scientist Journal, freeze frame fiction, and other publications. Visit her website at www.sylviaheike.com or find her on Twitter @sylviaheike.

I'm bending the rules of the Brotherhood just entering the Museum of Recent History, but I must pay my respects. Whoever invented this—presenting history barely a few weeks old in a museum—must be delighted. A fresh tragedy means something new to put on display and charge for.

The queue moves slowly as if hinting I can still turn back. When my turn comes, I slide a crumpled note over the counter and grab my sticker. I peel off the back and place it on the collar of my shirt—grey and unremarkable in every way, just like me. *The First Tenet: To be unseen, a Brother must hide in plain sight.*

No one will recognise me or even know I was here, and it's a blessing since the force that pulled me here is guilt.

I trail an older couple into the exhibition hall. Tourists. The woman's faded eyes fill with sparks of awe. She bites her lip, attempting to hide her inappropriate excitement. The man's fingers curve around his camera bag. For them, there are no nightmares here, only a personal rush.   I pass the couple so I can begin at the end. It's safer that way in case I want to make an early exit.

Everywhere around me lies familiar memorabilia in all its macabre glory: bits and pieces from aboard the MS Peregrine where a simple assassination at a birthday party escalated into a massacre. Extravagant ball gowns and black suits stand suspended on pedestals, the only bodies inside them ghosts. Their glass displays bear a striking resemblance to glass coffins. Around each hole in the expensive fabric, I spot copious amounts of dried blood.

A sign has been attached to each display, and one by one, I make acquaintance with a laminated face and a name to go with it. Their faces, joyful like this, are foreign to me. Aboard the ship, everyone wore fancy party masks, but even when I examine the lips, the chins, the dimples, they all look the same. Anonymous like me.

All but one. Aleksandr Callis, the intended target. He was infected, and there's no disease more devastating than global greed. The brotherhood had no choice but to stop him.

The events of the night still play in my mind. I served drinks, pacing to the live orchestrated music. The guests danced and whirled while Aleksandr sat watching, flanked by his body-guards. Against instructions, Brother August took the shot in the open, drawing attention. I neutralised one of the guards before my tray of champagne flutes touched the floor. After that, general panic hit the room, and the guests got caught in the crossfire.

Seventeen people died that night. The Brotherhood is responsible, no matter whose bullets they were.

I take a deep breath and push back the red hot blanket of anger and regret. I remind myself why I'm here. Staring into the bright eyes of Aleksandr's younger self, I say a silent prayer for each victim, each interrupted life. I save the last prayer for Aleksandr. *The Second Tenet: To honour life, a Brother must respect every life, even those he takes.*

I start toward the exit, threading past the exhibits—chairs, life jackets, ship railings—anything that could be pried loose has been brought here for show. It wouldn't surprise me if the bullets carved out from the flesh of the victims are on display, too.

My mind drifts to an unmarked grave and a man in it. No

sign of him here; the brotherhood made sure of it. May Brother August rest in peace.

A group of people dressed in black flow into the exhibition hall, their faces ghostly pale. I recognise their masks of grief.

These are the families of the victims and a few of them walk with crutches, survivors themselves. I keep my head low and feign interest in a fruit bowl that sits on a marble stand. How could these people have any desire to be here, to witness this farce?

I give them quick glances, waiting for them to pass. My gaze locks onto a man lingering behind them. I know him. What business does another Brother have here? The crowd moves forward, exposing him. He's not with them, only pretending. A trick I once taught him, but I can't believe how far he's pushing it. And to what end?

I edge closer. A piece of the ship's hardwood panelling, adorned with bullet holes and propped up in the middle of the room, separates us. He cocks his head, focused on the exhibits. His every feature is confident, unfettered. I see no honour, no remorse.

He smiles.

Fortunately for him, I'm not carrying a weapon or I would be tempted to break every rule to enforce just one. *The Third Tenet: To reform the Brotherhood, a Brother must strike like a serpent, even at his own Brother. Not the last of the tenets, but it will be for him.*

I drop the sticker into a trash bin on my way out. He won't see it coming. I was never here.

THANK YOU

Many thanks to our patrons
and supporters, especially:

KE JAECK
TORY HOKE

Want to see your name here? Become a patron!
patreon.com/lunastation
 patreon

ABOUT THE COVER

MARY WOLLSTONECRAFT SHELLEY

Widely acknowledged as the mother of all science fiction that came after her most famous novel, "Frankenstein", Mary Shelley was notable in her own time both for her work as a writer and her radical feminist views, inherited in part from her mother. Despite later being downplayed as simply the wife of Percy Bysshe Shelley, Mary Shelley's own contributions as an editor, writer, and political thinker have returned to the spotlight and she is once more viewed as a force of intelligence and creativity equal to that of her husband and other male friends and relations.

ERIN DEMOSS

Erin is a graphic designer from Oklahoma who geeks out over typography and information design. She has been interested in art all her life and fell in love with graphic design and illustration while going to school for public relations. She is a cat lady, a Leo, and a Star Wars nut. Her favorite book is American Gods by Neil Gaiman and her spirit animal is Louise Belcher.

You can find more of her work at erindemoss.com

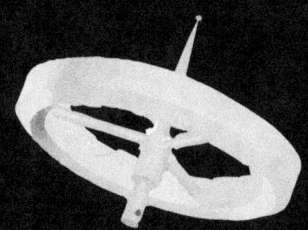